AMERICAN SKIN

AMERICAN SKIN

A NOVEL BY
KEN BRUEN

KATE'S MYSTERY BOOKS
JUSTIN, CHARLES & CO. PUBLISHERS
BOSTON

FIRST EDITION 2006

This is work of fiction. All characters and events portrayed in this
work are either fictitious or are used fictitiously.

Library of Congress Cataloging-in-Publication Data is available.

Published in the United States by Kate's Mystery Books,
an imprint of Justin, Charles & Co., Publishers,
www.justincharles.com
Distributed by National Book Network, Lanham, Maryland
www.nbnbooks.com

1 2 3 4 5 6 7 8 9 10

Printed in the United States of America

Book design by Boskydell Studio

For Eoin Colfer, who writes the
books the world reads
and
McKenna Jordan and David Thompson
who sell the books the world
should read at Murder By the Book,
in Houston, Texas

Glossary of Irish Words, Expressions and Irish-English Usage. Irish-English is as different from The Queen's English as a pint of Guinness is to a pint of Bitter. The former is as dark as the latter is weak.

Agus a mhathair: And His mother
Agus bheannacht: And blessings
Airgead: Money
Bangers: Sausage/secondhand car
Banjaxed: Fucked
Bhi curamach: Be careful/mind yourself
Bollocks: See bowsie
Boreen: Small unpaved road
Bowsie: Thug/shithead/accountant
Bringlodi: Dreams
Ceili: Irish music festival
Crack: Fun . . . party time
Culchie: Anyone not from Dublin (not flattering)

Currachs: Boats used by the Aran slanders

Cute hoor: Smart-ass

Dia leat: God be with you

Dubh: Black

Ejit: See bollix

Feck: The polite form of fuck

Filum: Movie

Fuaraigh: Chill (out)

Gobshite: A bollix with notions

Gra go mor: Mega love

Gunna: Gun

Gurrier: Thug

Kybosh: Jinx

Leat fein: You, too

Mobile: Cell phone

Notion: Ego inflation

Och ocon: Woe is me

Oul wan: Old woman

Pg mo thoin: Kiss my ass

Pishrog: Belief or expression based on superstition

Ride and a rasher: Sex followed by breakfast

Shebeens: Illegal drinking clubs

Sin sceal eile: That's a whole other story

Slainte: Cheers

Slainte amach: Cheers with feeling

Smashing: Terrific

Sneachta: Snow

Ta tu aras: You're back . . . couldn't cut it, huh?

The Boyos: The IRA

Wan/yer wan: A woman, derogatory term in heavy Galway
accent

THE TRIBES OF GALWAY were fourteen merchant families who settled in the town between the 1230s and the 1540s and who held power and prestige until the early decades of the twentieth century. They were not tribes in the usual sense. The term was apparently adopted by the townspeople themselves or used as a derisive term by Cromwellian soldiers.

Among the most ferocious of the tribes were the Blakes . . . famed as soldiers.

The Browns — no mean fighters, either — are sometimes known as Bruen.

One of the first casualties at Gettysburg was a D. Bruen. A Richard Bruen is reputed to have skinned his enemies. Richard respected and feared a local warlord and eventually killed him. Donning the skin, he tried to literally become the man he'd admired.

DIVORCE

GLEN TRIED to keep the SUV steady. It was the oldest
model, lacked the safety features of the newer ones; not
even the seat belts were secure and Karen had been on
Glen's case about how unsafe it was, but with his drinking,
he'd let it slide, like everything else.

He'd sworn to get it adjusted now he was sober but they
had to run . . . right now.

The needle was hitting 100 and Karen was screaming,

"He's right on us."

Glen, sweat pouring into his eyes, shouted,

"Goddamn it, Kar, I can't risk going off the road."

The vehicle on their rear was blinding them with mega
lights. Behind Karen, Rosie, their four-year-old daughter,
was staring saucer eyed at her parents; she'd never heard
them cuss each other. Beside her was Ben, ten years old,
wearing a Jet shirt, his father's old catcher's mitt in his lap.
He pulled at it, as if it might end the terror. Glen felt the

chassis sway dangerously; if a car came from the other direction, they were fucked. He was hogging the middle of the road as it was. Karen, near hysteria, howled,

"Glen . . ."

Rosie tried to cover her ears; her mother's fear frightened her more than the bogey man behind. The man behind popped a Juicy Fruit, hit the volume on the stereo, The Clash with "London's Burning."

He was in his late forties, wearing tooled cowboy boots, faded 501s, and a Lakers shirt. A jagged scar on his left cheek resembled a lightning strike. A whore in Philly, whom he'd tried to cheat out of her fee, had come at him with a broken bottle, attempting to gouge his eye out. He'd beaten her to an inch of her life then fucked her again, all the time, the blood pouring from the slash she'd inflicted. He was proud of it now, told folk it happened in the First Desert Storm, a raghead had tried to take him out. On his left arm was a tattoo with the name "Dade" . . . a souvenir of a time he'd been incarcerated down in Dade County; of all his jail time, it was the most fun, he got to kick the shit out of a drag queen and the food was fine, hash browns, gravy, grits, and mashed potatoes, with pecan pie to follow. On the seat was a Walther PPK. He fastened his foot on the accelerator, the grill on his truck jolting the tail of the SUV. He reached on the dash for his Kools, one fluid motion, working the cig into his mouth and flicking a Zippo, bearing the logo "1st Airborne."

He'd bought it off a guy in Tijuana.

He glanced at the weapon, the butt was custom fitted and he touched it, muttered,

"Lock and load."

A snapshot of Tammy Wynette hung from the mirror, tied with an Indian braid. He grinned at her, pedal to the metal, having more fun than hunting bear in god's own country.

Karen, terror soaking her top, knew who was behind. When she first met him, he was the soul of charm. She and Glen were having a trial separation, see if the 12 Step program would work for him. Even now, she couldn't quite figure how the man had become so quickly part of their lives, as if he'd planned it. He was so good with her son, played ball with him, treated her like a princess, never raised his voice and, if anything, he was almost too good to be true.

He'd even offered to fix up the SUV, saying that old model was a real hazard.

As the pursuit intensified, she wished now she'd let him do that.

Then Glen returned, sober, quiet, and attentive, asking for one more chance. The kids were delighted and she'd agreed. Told Dade, and watched in astonishment as he said,

"Ain't gonna happen, lady."

The change in his voice, the change in his face, like a demon had been revealed.

Unnerved, she'd said,

"I never promised you this was going to develop into something."

Keeping her voice reasonable, though a fierce sense of dread was building, she just wanted him to go away. They'd been sitting in her kitchen, coffee mugs on the table and without any warning, he'd lifted a mug, hurled it through the window. The effortless power he's summoned without exerting himself. Her little girl had come running in and he said,

"Nothing to worry about sweet thing, Mom and Dad just having a little disagreement."

The little girl, who'd never taken to him, near spat,

"You're not my Daddy."

He tut-tutted, Karen had never in her life heard anyone actually make that sound. Turning his eyes full on Karen, he said,

"You've turned our little girl against me, her own Dad."

He managed to sound hurt and lethal. She realised he was completely crazy, that brand of insanity that is so extreme that it almost passes for normal. She said, trying for a firm tone,

"I think you better leave now."

He was on his feet, one fluid motion, towering over her, the Juicy Fruit's aroma all over her, asked,

"You're saying you want a divorce, that what you trying to tell me?"

And she'd lost it, shouted,

"You maniac, we're not married, get out of my house or I'll call the cops."

He did the worst thing, he smiled at her, a smile of such malevolence that she shuddered. He strolled towards the door, said,

"You're a bad lady."

Glen came back and for a little while, it seemed okay. Till Dade appeared in the driveway, a gun in his hand, and began shooting. They'd done the only thing they could, they jumped in the SUV and fled. Karen could see his face as Dade strolled towards the door, the smile in place, and from his truck she could hear that damn Tammy Wynette singing. Glen had asked as they burned rubber out of there,

"What does he want?"

Karen had told the truth,

"To kill us all."

There was no doubt in her mind.

Rosie, unable to bear the tension, reached for the door handle. Mum had cautioned her not to touch it till Daddy fixed it and the seat belt didn't even lock.

The shock of wind rocked Glen and he went,

"What the fuck?"

The man in the truck saw what appeared to be a package hurled from the SUV, bounce against his grill, and disappear. He ducked reflexively, nearly losing control.

Karen twisted round in her seat, moaned,

"Oh sweet Jesus."

Ben let the mitt go, the wind tearing into the seat. Karen grabbed at the wheel, screaming,

"Stop . . . stop . . ."

And the vehicle went off the road.

Crashed into a tree at a speed upwards of 120 mph. Karen, her air cushion not working, shot through the windshield, hitting the tree with her head, crushing the neck down into the torso. Glen's air cushion kicked in and he sank into its folds. Ben, his belt tied, the only one still working, bounced against the upholstery. The truck ploughed into them, the grill preventing serious damage. Dade's head hit the dash, opening a three-inch cut above his right eye. Blood began to pour down his face. Took him a few minutes to focus, then he reached under his seat, saying,

"Rocking."

Got a bandana, a souvenir from a Springsteen gig, wrapped it round his head, said,

"Sucker hurts."

The Clash had shut down with the collision, he said,

"Bummer Strummer."

A silence followed. He popped a couple reds, reached for the Walther, got out. His boots crunched on the asphalt as he sauntered towards the SUV. He surveyed the make of the thing, thinking it must have been the first off the line, how goddamn old was that? The lights from the ruined vehicle lit up the tree. He could see the remains of Karen, suspended on a branch, asked,

"Hanging out, babe?"

Glen pulled his head from the cushion, took in the carnage before him as the glass on his window shattered, a voice asking,

"Glen, how you doing there buddy, day at a time, that how it goes?"

Shot him twice in the upper chest, dragged him out, leaned over the seat, looked at Ben, took the mitt, and put a round in the child's face. Counted, said,

"Uh . . . huh, one missing."

A Buick approached, slowed, catching him in the glare, he moved to the side as the car stopped. An elderly man behind the wheel, rolling down the window, going,

"What happened?"

Dade shrugged, said,

"Shit happened."

Shot him between the eyes, reached in, got the wallet, had a hundred bucks in there. He climbed into the truck, reversed, a grinding of metal as the grill came free, pulled out, moved off, began to sing,

"Our D-I-V-O-R-C-E becomes final today, me and little J-o-e . . ."

His voice was low, modulated, almost a hint of sweetness in the tone.

His lights braked on a hill, then disappeared in the direction of Tucson.

"It's such a sad old feeling
the fields are soft and green.
it's memories that I'm stealing,
But you're innocent when you dream."

—TOM WAITS

Galway, Ireland

IT WAS TEN DAYS since the "heist." I'd been lying low, watching the news, wondering if I was about to be arrested. The smart thing would have been to stay put, let the heat fade. But I was antsy, anxious to move. When you're sitting on more money than you could ever even count, you're not too laid back. That my oldest friend died in the robbery was a burden I couldn't shake, refused to dwell on it.

Siobhan, my girl for a long time, came out of the kitchen, asked,

"Can we switch to *Sex and The City*, it's the final series."

I was glad to move, three beers hadn't mellowed me. I'd some Vicodin, the ultimate painkiller, but was saving them for the flight, said,

"Sure."

Siobhan was so Irish, she might have come from central casting, red hair, snub nose, fine body, and that white skin the Americans call "Irish Colour."

They know about colour.

I grabbed another beer and she asked,

"Will you watch with me?"

I could have but was finding it difficult to be still, said,

"It's always about shoes."

She laughed, the way women do when men "don't get it."

Which is most of the time.

One line did make me laugh. Carrie had a boy toy and said, "I don't know if I should blow him or burp him."

A bottle of Black Bushmills on the sink. We'd been keeping it for a special occasion. I guess this would have to be it. I put the beer down, broke the seal, got some heavy tumblers from the press, poured freely, she said,

"Put lemonade in mine."

Christ, what a travesty. But it hardly seemed the time to mention that. I poured the lemonade, made a mental note to call it "pop," get into American mode. Every day, I adjusted my vocabulary, getting in gear.

The robbery flashed across my mind, Tommy's ruined face, the bullet hole where his nose had been, and gripped the counter, muttered,

"Motherfucker."

Siobhan turned, asked,

"What?"

"Nothing, caught my finger on the cap, no big thing."

I meant Stapleton, the coldest man I ever met. Our third member of the gang, he was the iceman, with eyes like the dead, according to rumour, and a long time with paramilitaries. He'd supplied the weapons, most of the strategy.

He also shot Tommy.

In bed, Siobhan asked me if I loved her, I said I did.

Kept it casual, I loved her more than mere words could express, she was the beat of my heart.

She worked for an investment bank, was helping me off load, legitimise the mountain of cash. I already had American Express, Mastercard, Visa . . . Gold.

And a healthy wedge of dollars. Siobhan had a banker's attitude toward money, not concerned where it came from but very anxious where it was going, I'd asked,

"Are you sure you won't get caught, this is a serious amount of cash you're channelling?"

Got the look, she said,

"The day a bank refuses money is the end of democracy as we know it."

It was in my interest to agree. I'd been worried about CAB, the Criminal Assets Bureau, who were highly effective in shutting down John Gilligan and a legion of others. She explained,

"They've been bringing down dopers, now they're after politicians."

Pause.

She held my face, staring intently, asked,

"You're not political are you Steve?"

Like most Irish men I could talk it, give me a few pints, I might even mean it. I just rarely bothered to vote.

Our plan was to meet up in Tucson, picked the eighth day in the month as it was, she said, her lucky number. I'd given Siobhan a gold Miraculous Medal, with a long chain, seemed in keeping with our rendezvous, lucky numbers and religion, how could we lose?

Before I left the next morning, she'd suddenly taken it off, hung it round my neck, a serious expression clouding her face. I'd asked,

"Why?"

"I have a terrible feeling you're going to need it."

She was right.

It was Siobhan who'd chosen Tucson and naturally I asked why. First she said,

"That dry heat, every day being warm."

It may seem to other nationalities that we're more than a little obsessed with the rain. We are.

If you spend a childhood getting drenched, soaked to the skin, wet to your very core, you'd be happy never to see a drop of it again. When we get, say, five, yeah, count 'em, five days of sunshine for a summer, we're near orgasmic. We must be one of the few nations who hope global warming is true if it means dry weather. Then she said,

"And you'll want to see where that gunfight took place."

Jesus, I hadn't the heart to tell her she'd got the wrong town. Loving someone does mean not correcting them. Shortly before I left, she discovered her error, asked me why I'd said nothing, and I did the one thing she respected most of all, I told the truth, said,

"I didn't want you to feel bad."

Her expression, of wonder, awe, then she said,

"So it's true, there are men who really love women."

To change the subject I asked,

"Are we going to Tombstone then?"

She shuddered, blessed herself then,

"Good god no . . . we couldn't live in a place named after a graveyard."

The awful irony is that we may as well have chosen it: Graves were going to be the legacy of the whole enterprise in the fallout.

"Who by Fire"

— LEONARD COHEN

DADE HAD DISCOVERED Tammy Wynette in prison, he'd done more time inside than he liked to remember. As a child, he'd been nourished, cared for, by parents who adored him. He was the exception to the rule that if a child is reared with love and warmth, he'll be a mature, compassionate adult. But then, Dade was a force of nature, as vicious, cold, and unconcerned as the storms that arise out of nowhere and drown the fishermen travelling on the currachs to the Aran Islands. The islanders are so fatalistic about this eventuality that they never learn to swim.

Meeting Dade, you were in a similiar position, any survival skills you'd attained weren't going to be much help. He was the Great White shark of urban malaise: random, ferocious, and struck from the depths of unfathomable darkness. His earliest memory was killing a goldfish; a birthday present, he snatched it from the bowl, threw it in the toilet, watched it swim for a bit, then poured bleach in.

The tiny creature writhing in agony exhilarated Dade and he took the plunger, poked the fish till it near disintegrated from the cleanser. His mother, discovering the perform-ance, was horrified and gave him a serious talk. He learned to lie almost instantly, claiming he was trying to . . . *clean the little fishy.*

Then he immediately learned another vital skill, weep-ing. As the tears flowed, he felt nothing, save a buzz from fucking with another person. His father was less gullible and Dade noticed him watching him from then on. Next birthday, he got a puppy, a beautiful collie that his Mom suggested they call Lassie. Dade torched Lassie; it took a time and he got bit twice but felt it was a fair tradeoff for the sheer elation. This time, he was taken to a doctor; alas it was too late to take Lassie anywhere save the trash.

The doctor managed to get under Dade's skin and for the first time in his professional career, was scared. He'd al-ways taken the view that pure evil belonged to movies like *The Omen*, to books from Stephen King; he adhered to the theory that nurture and/or chemistry was the root of most psychosis. Dade changed all that.

Ten years old and the vibe emanating from this child sent shivers up the doctor's spine. What was worse was the kid knew the effect he had, saw the look in the doctor's eyes and promised,

"You send me away, I'll get out and find you."

It was nonsense, a kid threatening a highly qualified physician. But who needed the aggravation? With a bit of luck, the kid would follow his instincts and be locked in a maximum pen for the rest of his life. So he prescribed pills. He did say to the father,

"That child will need watching."

The father stared at the doctor, asked,

"For three hundred bucks an hour you're telling me something new?"

The doctor, sensing malpractice, tried,

"He'll probably grow out if it."

The father didn't doubt it, said,

"I'm sure he will grow, but into what, you want to tell me that?"

The doctor didn't.

The person who benefited from the session was Dade; he learned two things, power and secrecy. The keys to the dark kingdom. As he grew and more animals disappeared from the neighbourhood, he learned to cover his tracks. When he was fifteen, his father, in a last-ditch effort to help his son, took him fishing. Big mistake.

It took Dade nearly ten minutes to drown his Dad but he did prolong it just a tad, for the hell of it and for payback. He'd mastered the art of mimicry and knew how to fake grief, so to all, he appeared inconsolable. His mother knew but she had found her own dark realm, booze, in the shape of vodka martinis. Get a pitcher of those babies ready by noon and you weren't hurting at all. She hung herself on Dade's seventeenth birthday, and Dade hit the road. He'd always refer to his upbringing as idyllic, and it was: If you were a psycho and didn't get caught, where was the down side?

Movies, Dade loved 'em. Peckinpah, Tarantino, Oliver Stone, those guys rocked. Driving through the small towns of the Midwest, he'd check the local movie house and if one of those guys had a movie up, he'd pull in, buy a ticket, a shitload of popcorn, sodas, do a little crystal, get the mood right. Sitting there, he'd be in hog heaven. Times, too, in those little towns, he'd score some chickie, usually worked the soda fountain or waited tables in the diner. He'd give her his hundred-watt smile, lay all those Elvis-type manners on her, and drive her to a place outside town. If they fought back, he liked it that much better. Left them battered, bruised, and as close to dead as it gets. After, as they crouched, huddled in the road, he'd blow a kiss, caution,

"You all be careful out there, there's bad folk riding our highways."

Felt he'd aided their growth.

Above all, Dade loved America, you didn't need to tell him it was God's own country. Man, he was out there, proving it and if he was nearer to Satan than the Pale Nazarene, well, it was all part of the same cycle. Rock 'n' roll.

Early on he discovered The Clash . . . Joe Strummer was the man. For a while he adopted an English accent but got tired of it, it was hard to ask for grits and eggs over easy in Brit prissy tone. Plus, some of the good ol' boys interpreted it as homosexual, and that was not to be recommended in Bible country.

In Sausalito, Dade came across one of those new age shops. It tickled him that it was spelled *Shoppe*. He said to the aging hippie who tended the counter,

"Need to learn to spell, buddy."

There was a host of angels on every side, and U2 was on the soundtrack, with "If Will Send His Angels." America was in the grip of angelic fever then, Danny DeVito had proclaimed his success due to his guardian angel; the best-seller list was full of titles like, *Getting to Know Your Angel.*

Dade thought it was full of shit. The hippie stared at him. Dade was wearing a long black duster, his perennial cowboy boots, and a T-shirt with "Never mind the Bollocks . . ." In his waistband was a SIG, locked and loaded. Dade had his Ray Bans on and the guy couldn't see his eyes, so he didn't know what he was dealing with, he asked,

"Do you know the name of your angel?"

Dade hadn't yet discovered Tammy or he'd have said her. He looked at the guy, adjusted his Bans, asked,

"You fuckin' with me buddy?"

The hippie, full of love, peace, and other good karma, didn't cuss or ever raise his voice, had just done a bong and was way mellow, said,

"My angel's name is Aine . . . that's, like, Gaelic."

Dade loved this, rarely did he meet an out-and-out fruiter and he sure liked to play, he said,

"That's, like, a crock, man."

He leaned heavy on the *man*, get the Woodstock buzz up there. In his head The Clash was unreeling with "Straight to Hell," and he could feel his mojo pumping . . . he knew "Trash City" would automatically follow. He glanced round the shop, there were lots of Dungeons & Dragons figurines interspersed with the angels, the hippie was clearly an equal opportunity employer or just lazy. Dade spotted a Buddha, incongruous among the other stuff, asked,

"What's with the small fat dude?"

The hippie sighed, explained,

"That's Prajnaparamita, who contemplates the essence of nothing."

Dade was excited, he didn't know why but it sang to him, said,

"How much?"

The hippy, sensing a sale, got hot, asked,

"You don't want an angel as well?"

Dade could turn on a nickel, one moment, he was your best buddy then he'd a knife at your throat, he was turning fast, asked,

"You deaf, I asked you the goddamn price you fuck, I want a angel, I'll reach over, grab me one, I'm getting through to you?

He was, and the price for the Buddha was steep but Dade had recently hit a 7-Eleven, handed over half the freight. The hippie began to wrap it and Dade snapped,

"Don't bother."

He set the little fat fella on his dash, made him happy. When he got busted later and did the hard time, the Buddha disappeared but by then, Dade had the concept of nothingness ingrained in his heart, he didn't need a figurine to remind him.

You wanted to set Dade off, and it wasn't a difficult task at the best of times, mention Texas. He'd done a stretch, among his first, in Huntsville and learned that the Lone Star State was not kind to inmates. The warden telling him,

"Y'all the crap I wipe on my boot and you know what, boy?"

Dade didn't know squat then, his education was only beginning, and he muttered that no, he didn't. The warden had given him a full-voltage smile, which Dade was to learn was the worst of bad news. Those guys smiling at you, you were in line for whooping hurt. The warden explained,

"I'm a good ol' Texas boy, like to keep my boots spit and shined, you gonna be messing with my footwear while you're my guest?"

Dade swore he wouldn't.

It was a hard year, he learned the meaning of retaliate first, and it was not something he ever forgot. Leaving Texas, the troopers warned,

"You don't come back, boy."

He planned on staying the hell away.

A movie Dade saw, *The Stepfather*, set off a bomb in his head, not that it needed much to ignite his already frenzied brain, it was about a psycho who literally adopts a family, and becomes the American dream.

For a time.

Then he slaughters them.

Dade wasn't sure which he liked best, the instant family and all the values he'd never have or the massacre. But the concept lodged. Meet a divorcée with kids, then charm your way in, have the whole package for a few months, play with that gig, and then pull the plug. When he took the heavy fall and did the long stretch, it was this vision that got him through many riots, lockdown behind the walls. He even had a faded snapshot of a woman with two kids, it came with a cheap wallet he bought in Reno, the divorce capital. Somehow, it survived his strip search, the trip to the pen. He showed it to various inmates and it bought him a certain amount of kudos, the most dangerous motherfuckers on the planet got soppy when confronted with this.

Go figure.

Over time, he came to believe it was actually real, so when he did meet Karen, it was like he'd had her all those years. Her boy had a baseball mitt and Dade shouted,

"What about them Mets?"

Got a blank look from the kid.

But he learned, took it easy, slow and measured, charm oozing from every pore. The little girl, she never bought his act, plus, she missed her real dad. Glen, her dad, was a drunk but had entered a 12 Step program, was putting his act together, intended reclaiming his family.

Dade was never, never going to let anyone, anytime, anywhere take something away from him. In prison, they'd taken away near all he put value on but he'd found a whole new set of, if not values, then priorities, and chief among them was, if they fuck with you, you get medieval on their ass. Real simple in Dade's mind, they didn't want to live with him, they didn't want to live.

Do the math.

House invasions were becoming increasingly more frequent in the heartland; even Ohio, the setting for electoral confusion and aggravation, saw gangs storming into homes, laying waste. Dade felt he'd brought a new slant to the art: car invasion. Wipe the vehicle, the occupants, the whole nine, clean off the earth. Put that in yer car commercials.

Dade had come late to Shane MacGowan, the punk era. The Pogues happened while he was inside and the music of the tiers was either Johnny Cash, gangsta rap, or Mex whining. In a diner way down in the Bayou, he'd heard "Fairytale of New York" . . . and been riveted. Kirsty Mac-Coll with Shane MacGowan. Later, he found the video, the black-and-white one with the NYPD singing ". . . Galway Bay." Dade knew Galway from shinola but went out and bought a Claddagh ring. Lost the damn thing in a tussle with some bikers near Fresno. They'd been trying to take his finger but settled for the Irish wedding band. Dade hated Angels.

That one of them was riding low on his bike with Dade's ring would be a slow and slower burn. When the shitstorm went down later, with the one named Fer, it was real personal for Dade.

In his mind, the Angels and Shane MacGowan were linked, it made little sense but rationale was never top of his agenda. He's scoured magazines for references to Mac-Gowan . . . adored a piece he read by Suggs of the group Madness.

"I remember seeing Shane a few years aback and he said . . . I can't talk now, I'm doing an interview."

Hours later, the interviewer staggered out, having been drowned in about nineteen bottles of wine, his bag hanging open and fuck all in his notebook. Dade would have given a lot to see the bold Shane in concert but The Pogue's hey-day was nigh done when Dade got out of the penitentiary. Still, he imagined what it would have been like to attend concerts such as the infamous one titled Hell's Ditch Party.

That Dade would relinquish Shane, and others like Johnny Cash for Tammy Wynette was a remarkable about-face, even for a chameleon like him. A bottle of tequila and a botched attempt at housebreaking were the catalysts that brought Dade to his love of the blond singer.

"Buying the farm" was a euphenism for death that Dade liked, had used it his own self, going, *dude bought the farm*. The Farm in Angola would rid him of that. When he was sentenced there, the guys in the holding pen with him, said,

"You're dead, motherfucker."

The stories of rape, brutality, murder, were legion and that was just from the Guards. The inmates were the meanest collection of dangerous men ever assembled in one place. Dade's lawyer, one of the free legal aid brigade, suggested to Dade the night before he made the trip,

"Try and get hold of a rope, or some sheets."

Dade, confused, asked,

"You think I can escape?"

The lawyer, young but already with eyes of glass, said,

"No, I'm saying you should take the easy way out."

Over the years on The Farm, there were a lot of times that Dade regretted not taking the advice.

He went in there with a very dangerous past, a liking for violence of the extreme variety. When he finally got released, that was still in place but the difference was, it was honed, focused, and oh, so very lethal.

LAND OF THE FREE,
HOME OF THE BRAVE

E.B.WHITE WROTE of New York:

"No one should come to live in New York unless he is willing to be lucky."

Man, I was willing and I was certainly dressed for it. Wearing a lightweight navy suit — cost an arm and a leg but guaranteed not to crease. I wanted to hit American Immigration like a citizen. Post 9/11, checks were going to be intense. Got the flight from Galway to Dublin first, packed with French shooters. Yes, armed French folk: They've been coming for years, weapons to the teeth and systematically decimating our wildlife. Another year, there wouldn't be a bird left in the countryside.

I was glad to lose them at Dublin and headed for duty free, bought a bottle of Bush, then filled out the forms for Immigration. Into the bar for a final pint of Guinness, the barman was a pro, let it sit for a good five minutes before he creamed it off. I'd just taken a sip when the announcement

"U.S. Immigration is now open."

The old saying, *If you leave anything behind, make sure it's dark*. I felt a wave of apprehension, if they turned me down, I was in deep shit. But it went like a breeze, the officer asked,

"Business or vacation?

I said vacation and got the 90 day visa with,

"You have a real good trip."

I had two Vicodin, the bottle of Bush, a shitpile of cash, how could I not? I said,

"Thanks very much."

I'd been tempted to go first class but had to keep a low profile, so economy it was. The seats were narrow, your knees jammed against the one ahead. If they let it tilt after takeoff, I'd be sandwiched. A nun took the seat beside me, a large silver cross dangling on her front. I never know how to address them, "Sister" sounds like *Boyz in the Hood*, keep it neutral, went,

"Good afternoon."

Got a brief smile. Suited me, I didn't want chat. The stewardess gave us the safety drill and seemed very angry in her delivery, probably as we weren't listening. Then we were airborne and I looked out the window, wondering if I'd ever return, decided to try my new accent, said,

"Gee, Ireland is so green."

She was surprised, asked,

"You're American?"

"Yes, ma'am."

I didn't know if a nun was a good omen or not. If we crashed, at least I was next to a silver crucifix. The drinks cart came. It was no longer free, you had to pay and through the nose. The nun was looking longingly at the display but the tariff had caused her to demur. I used the moment to dry swallow a vike, asked,

"Ma'am, I'd be honored to treat you."

Her face lit up but still,

"Oh, I don't know."

I went for the sucker punch, said,

"I sure as shooting hate to drink alone."

A line the French might appreciate.

Cringed a bit, I was too eager, overdoing the accent and worse, my Irish was leaking all over the intonation, needed work. If she'd picked up, she didn't comment, said,

"Well, I will so, may I have a red wine?"

Ordered that and a large Jameson, water back. Passed over a twenty euro note and got Dixie in change. See how I've meshed those Americanisms in there. Now if I could only just goddam "walk the walk." I touched my glass to hers, said,

"Slainte."

Mangled it as best I could and got a radiant smile, all lightness. She said,

"Lovely pronunciation."

Signed, sealed and near delivered. I knocked back the whiskey, said,

"If I'm asleep when they serve dinner, don't wake me."

She took a sip of the wine, said,

"I wouldn't dream of it."

I closed my eyes, was gone, it seemed but a moment. Put it down to the Vicodin but I had a dream of such reality, it was like truth. More like a total recollection. The night I met Siobhan, I'd been on a real downer. Tommy was acting the bollocks as usual, drinking his face off, making a nuisance of himself, and generally getting on my nerves. I'd been feeling sorry for myself, the constant Galway rain was showing no sign of letup, we'd had two weeks of incessant downpour. The adjective "teeming" was designed for our climate. It lashed down, relentless, soaking you through, why we drank so much whiskey, and because we liked the stuff. My life seemed to have hit a cul-de-sac and no signpost on the horizon. Tommy had said,

"Let's go to a dance."

Yeah, right.

Just what I needed, a frigging ballroom. Surly Irish men herded one side, glaring at the women as if they hated them. To hear the women tell it, they did. It was a throwback to the old days, when our parents had no other diversion but the one Saturday night outing. We were spoilt for choice, the new Ireland of clubs, money, endless credit. The showbands had been the staple of the sixties, six to eight guys, blazers, white pants, bad hairpieces and worse music, usually covers of Elvis, Buddy Holly, and the Beach Boys. My father had explained,

"We danced our way through poverty."

It was meant to be a form of irony that there'd been a revival. The showbands were enjoying a renaissance, and Ecstasy had sure given us a thirst of dancing and late night revels. Young people wore suits and the women, what my mother used to call frocks. Fifties hairdoes that seemed to match the frocks and the guys, with the dark suits and gel in the hair. The only thing that didn't change was the bands, younger maybe and atrocious. Part of the irony. Who was the joke on when you pay to hear bad music?

Music is the passion of my life. Tom Waits, Johnny Cash, Tom Russell, Gretchen Peters, to name but the first line of my favourites. And at a reach, the Beach Boys. Our parents had snuck flasks of Jameson into the ballrooms. Our generation, cool and poised, because of the E, had a ferocious demand for bottled water. Tommy being the exception, he had a flask, not because of tradition but out of need. The band, all in their twenties, was murdering "Tell Laura I Love Her." I was hating every moment when Tommy sidled up to me, offered the flask, asked,

"Wanna hit?"

The lead vocalist had announced,

"Ladies' choice."

I knew from my father that this was the Irish male's nightmare. This was when you were glad you'd fortified the flask with double measures.

Tommy slunk off to score some dope — not a woman, the weed. I was looking at my watch, as if I had a pressing engagement. You're in a dance hall and you have a pressing appointment?

Who was I kidding?

The alternative was to watch the women give you that ice-cool appraisal and find you wanting. I was regretting not taking a shot of the Jameson, a big shot when I heard,

"Like to dance?"

I didn't answer, more out of surprise than rudeness though that was part of it. I'd my granite face on, the one that says,

"Hey, you don't wanna dance with me . . . like I give a shit?"

I turned and there was the caricature Irish colleen,

straight from central casting. No fooling, like an under-study for Maureen O'Hara. Red hair, wild and untamed, fresh complexion that screamed health. A small build, though finely shaped, very fine. Her face wasn't pretty, all the right features in place but something just missed mak-ing it so. What it was, was compelling, due to the vivacity of her eyes. I'm Irish, I've seen blue eyes all my life but here, here was blue like a kick in the gut. She smiled and I was lost, and delivered. She repeated,

"Wanna dance?"

And Mr/ Smooth, Mr/ Silver Tongued devil, said,

"Me?"

Irish women have great strength, and I was to see the very first show of it as she took my arm, said,

"The song will be over if you stand there debating."

And I smelled her perfume, like all the clichés, it en-veloped me. I walked on her feet, like twice and she said,

"We're going to have to show you a few steps, fellah."

Of all the things she'd say to me, none would quite have the resonance of that. The promise of a future implied. Control, reserve, lock down, these are the qualities or lia-bilities I've strived for. All out the damn window even be-fore I knew her name. I loved her right then and if the love deepened as it did and did, there were few moments to equal the dizzying exhileration of falling completely and utterly. Next song up was Alison Krauss and Brad Paisley's "Whiskey Lullaby." I know, it's pure schmaltz, pap as the Brits say, but never, and I mean never did I relish a song so much. She moved in close, put her hands round my waist, and I must have given a slight tremor as she said,

"Me too, that song speaks to me."

The song ended and I asked if she'd like a drink and she went,

"I'm parched."

I got the drinks and we sat on the balcony, I asked,

"What's your name?"

"Siobhan Keane and you're Stephen Blake, I know all belong to you."

Doesn't get more Irish than that.

The next dance was fast and we watched the couples jiving. Americans, when they hear this, ask, what?

"They're talking like black people? And why?"

No, they're dancing, it's our version of swing. And the women are experts, the guys are mainly terrified and truly, for once, are along for the ride. You want to observe a terrified Irishman, see his face as he goes into the first swing of the routine. Like all real macho men, I can't dance. Never mind the Micheal Flatley hype, he's Irish American, anyway, the way we tell it, only homosexuals can dance.

You'd believe we're kidding when we say this.

We're not.

My mother was a hell of a dancer and my father, he could fake it, a bit, sufficient for the odd wedding or wake, but you could never accuse him of enjoying it. Siobhan asked,

"You don't, I suppose, want to try that?"

Before I could shake my head, she asked,

"So, are you going to ask me out or just sit there, work on your hard man expression?"

That's how we began. It was even better than I anticipated. She made me feel like a man I'd want to be. I always wished I could have been the guy she thought I was. She was certainly the woman I loved being with. Unlike the current rituals, we didn't hop into bed straightaway. She said,

"I want to wait."

Fine by me as I was nervous, for the first time in my life, it mattered to me that it be special. Truth, too, I was afraid I'd disappoint her.

Gradually, I learned about her family. Her old man was a bad bastard. Drunk and vicious with it. He started out mean and the booze just fine-lined it. I never really got the full impact of the description *surly* till I met him. Siobhan had deferred for ages bringing me to her home. I'd rag her,

"What? You're ashamed of me?"

Then saw her face, the despair, the hurt and she said,

"No, I'm ashamed of them."

You never hear that in Ireland. No matter how bad the situation, the unit of family gets defended even when the evidence is in full sight. For her to say this cost her in ways even I didn't full realise. Trying for levity, which was among my more blind moments, I said,

"Jesus, how bad can they be?"

Her forehead furrowed in concentration, she went,

"The worst, and don't take the Lord's name in vain."

She told me of her brother, in jail for burglary, her sister with two kids before she was nineteen, a mother on pills. Or on tablets, as she put it. You don't hear that anymore, tablets, like something Moses bequeathed. My own mother was known to suffer from *nerves*. This was said with an almost imperceptible wink. Translate as drink.

Siobhan's wrath, and fiery it was, was reserved for her father. Her face literally curled in on itself, her eyes like murder, her mouth, tight and compressed as she recounted the beatings, the poverty, the sheer calculated cruelty of the man. I loved my own father and was at a loss to grasp that some men are just born bad and enjoy it.

Siobhan's mantra was money . . . you have money, you get out. She had no hang-up about where it came from, she worked in a bank and often said,

"Money has no conscience."

When I finally met her family, they were marginally worse than she'd described. They lived in what is laughingly referred to as genteel poverty. Trust me, there is nothing fucking genteel about being poor. In Ireland, translate as, they had nothing but they were clean. The house was part of a terrace, you could hear the people next door and they were loud. Not as loud as Siobhan's father.

From all she'd said, I anticipated a large, burly guy. He was a small shite, small in every sense, especially his actions. Met us at the door, dressed in unironed pants of a suit, an open-necked shirt that showed grey hair spouting at the throat. His hair was in deep recession, like the economy, and he had the eyes of a ferret, a can of beer in his hand, his greeting was,

"Lady Muck deigned to visit."

She stared at him for a moment then said,

"Thanks for dressing up, Dad."

He gave a laugh that had no relation to warmth or humour, went,

"Dress up, for your fancy man? Who have we this time, another merchant banker?"

And he laughed at his term, like we might not get the reference to what it rhymed with. I put out my hand and he looked at it as if I'd asked him for a fiver, said,

"You know where you can stick that."

That was the high point of the evening. We stayed all of twenty minutes, Siobhan's mother was in the front room, hugging her knees, she had the eyes of someone who got a terrible fright and never recovered. The conversation consisted of sneers from her dad, tiny whimpers from the mother. As we got up to leave, I noticed Siobhan slip some money to her mother who took it like salvation. Her father stood at the door with me, asked,

"You getting some?"

Took me a moment to grasp his implication then I turned, whispered,

"Some day, maybe we'll meet down the town, just you and me, I'll let you have *some*."

Like all bullies, he fell back on whining, said to the women,

"This piss head threatened me."

Siobhan was already moving to get away and I said to him,

"That wasn't a threat, that was a promise."

We were more than half way down the street when Siobhan said,

"Promise me you'll get me out of here."

I promised, having no idea how I'd accomplish that but it didn't seem the time to mention it.

JOHN A. STAPLETON

STAPLETON was built to last though the odds were against him. Brought up in Belfast in the real bad dark years, he saw his father murdered by the British army. He took to the streets early, dodging rubber bullets and worse. He displayed a natural talent for guerrilla tactics. The Falls road taught him all he ever needed to know about survival. The Boyos spotted his potential and he was carrying an Arma-Lite by the time he was fourteen. They sent him to south Armagh, bandit country, and for three years he harassed, terrorised, and laid down hell for the hapless squaddies assigned to that god forsaken territory.

He was commander of his own unit at the age of nineteen and seemed blessed by some deity to always evade capture. He regularly made the British army's top ten most wanted. Not all the touts, informers, or supergrasses could deliver him.

It was rumoured that his skills were fine-honed in the training camps of south Lebanon.

He was fuelled by a total hatred of all things English. Of short stature, he was wiry and began to attend gyms to build up muscle. Physical fitness was his passion and the key to his survival. Even his own mother said,

"God, he's an ugly child."

And he was, growing into an even uglier adult. He utilised that, letting his face intimidate people. A scar ran across his forehead, from the late detonation of a device in the centre of Derry. He'd never call it Londonderry. His nose had been broken more times than he could remember, due to literal in-fighting, up close and personal, the way he liked it. His street fighting was learned from the days of the Falls and consisted of fierce brutality combined with a speed that was near graceful in its execution. Face to face with some young soldier from the streets of Manchester, he liked nothing better than to drop his weapon, open his left palm and goad,

"Come on sissy boy."

He kept his head shaven and that, with his dark eyes, ruined features, made his opponents pause for that deadly second. All he needed.

The Peace Talks were like the worst news. He never wanted the hostilities to end, they were part of his very blood. He had joined a breakaway faction who continued to rob banks and cause mayhem. But he had been planning a heist down South for some time and just needed the right patsy. He wanted this on many levels. The attitude in the Republic towards the North pissed him off big-time. As if the situation didn't really concern them. When they got prosperous with the Celtic Tiger , they got even more arrogant. At least in his opinion. Sure, they had their poxy government bleating about Peace but you looked behind the earnest camera smiles and deep concern, you saw that they couldn't give a toss for the North. He'd make them care. Hit the fucks where it now mattered . . . in the wallet. Take down their banks, they'd notice. To add insult to injury, he wanted a Southerner involved and then he'd off the prick. From time to time, he'd lain low in Dublin and saw the response when his accent was aired. A slight hesitation, then the platitudes. What they wanted was for the North to fuck the hell off and stop bothering them. They had a world stage to Riverdance and didn't want it messed up with notions like freedom.

He'd conducted his own mini survey. Asked a selection of them to recite the Proclaimation of 1916 — not one bastard could. He was horrified, he could recite it in English and Irish. Nobody cared about the revival of the language, sure they had a TV channel catering to the native tongue but who watched it? The young kids were watching *The O.C. . . . The Simpsons . . . Fear Factor.*

He'd give them *Fear Factor,* all right. Try finding a pub with traditional music. Fuck no, all you got were U2 rip-off's. He'd nothing against U2, in fact he felt, "Where the Streets Have No Name" was one of the best songs ever about the conflict and Belfast in particular. The only Republican group worth the name, The Wolfe Tones, had broken up, didn't that say it all? He'd come of age in the sheebeens of Belfast, the illegal pubs in the no-go areas where night after night you got "The Men Behind the Wire," "The Ballad of Bobby Sands," "Brits Out," "This

Land is Your Land," real songs. With the bodhrans, spoons, accordions, Uilleann pipes, all blasting at mega warp.

Jesus, he'd been in a pub on Gardiner Street one night, a supposed Republican enclave in the heart of Dublin and a woman said to him,

"The Corrs are the heart of Ireland."

He'd muttered,

"Does it get more fucked than this?"

Van Morrison, before he got too rich and too arrogant, sang the wondrous "Madame George," that got John A. Stapleton as close to tears as even CS gas could achieve. In times of stress, like waiting on a rooftop, the lone sniper par excellence, he could sing the whole of *Astral Weeks* in his head. As his finger massaged the trigger, he'd sing,

"Saw you walking, up by Cypress Avenue. . . ."

As the Brit patrol arrived on the street below, and he selected the end soldier, fixed on him, he'd hum the melody of the final track on the album and blow the face apart. It was poetry, the music of his inheritance. And he'd disappear from the rooftop as silently as the sound of the album being shut down.

The first part of his name — John A; he never acknowledged John . . . it was the Irish form always . . . Sean; the "A" stood for St. Anthony, Stapleton believed firmly in the man. It was widely held that if you lost something, you made a deal with Anthony, say five euro to find your wallet. Stapleton was trying to figure out how much it would cost for a country. He figured Anthony had a whole better chance of finding a United Ireland than either the Irish or UK politicians.

Stapleton had an Achilles heel. Jameson. He could do

two shots tops. Once he hit three, he lost focus, became maudlin, sentimental, sloppy. He could down pints of the black all night and still take out a guy without any bother. Reach three Jameson and he started to talk. The worst action possible. You talked, you got shafted. He exercised massive control on the rare evenings he sampled the whiskey, as the two always loomed heavy for the third. Planning strategy, it was custom to plonk a bottle of the Jay on the table and get serious. Stapleton stuck to Guinness. More than once, a commander had asked,

"You don't drink spirits?"

Like heresy.

So he'd do the two, then reach for the stout. He made even the most hardened vets a little uneasy, they wondered why he never let his defences down, especially when they were in a safe house and could afford to let the pressure ebb. A time, they were holed up in Enniskillen, after three days of lockdown, one of the guys had asked,

"Don't you have a personal life?"

And got the look.

Stapleton flexed his fingers, always a dangerous sign, fixed his dark eyes on the guy, said,

"Let me set you straight on a couple of things."

The guy glanced round at the other members of the unit but they weren't getting into it, not with Stapleton. The guy wished he hadn't left his pistol in the bedroom as he heard,

"We're in a war sonny boy, not some damn picnic where you get the weekends off. I don't know who trained you, but they didn't do too good a job, else you wouldn't be asking questions. When Eire is free, when the last Brit is packing his arse out of our country, I'll start dating, having me some *fun.* . . ."

He paused, letting venom leak over the word, then,

"Meantime, we have a job to do, a sacred duty, like the martyrs of sixteen, we don't have time for *personal lives.* . . so shut your fucking mouth and get that pistol out of the bedroom, it won't do you a whole lot of good if the Paras come bursting in, you think they'll give you a moment to fetch it?"

The guy was killed two weeks later on a botched job in Derry, Stapleton shed no tears, muttered,

"Let that be a lesson to yous."

His legend was ensured when they captured a British major outside of Fermanagh. The man, a veteran of eighteen months on the streets of Belfast, had been taken at dawn, he was not intimidated by his captors, regarded them with scorn, so they sent Stapleton to have a wee chat with him.

The major was seated on a hard chair, a wooden table before him. Stapleton took the chair opposite, said,

"How are they treating you?"

The major had undergone extensive training in subversive warfare and was not impressed by the *good guy routine.* He reached into his tunic, extracted a pack of Rothmans, a gold Zippo, and fired up, blew the smoke at Stapleton. Stapleton didn't flinch, let the smoke invade his face, asked,

"Mind if I have one of these, I'm trying to quit but what the hell."

The major, control reined tight, pushed the pack over, said,

"Knock yourself out, Paddy."

Stapleton slowly lit the cig, studied the Zippo, it had the logo, "Queens finest." As Stapleton downed a lungful of smoke, like an addict who hasn't imbibed for a time, he asked, pointing at the logo,

"That a nancy boy thing?"

The major laughed, not quite believing this was the best the Boyos had to offer, said,

"You'd probably know, you look like a nancy boy yourself."

Stapleton gouged the cig into the major's right eye, saying,

"Jaysus, they're right, those yokes are bad for your health."

A few hours later, having garnered all the information the major had, he dragged the man outside, hung him from a tree near the road, said,

"It's a slow knot, going to take a while to croak."

He kept the Zippo, got a fellah on the Falls to erase the logo and put . . . "No Surrender" on there. It never ceased to amuse him that this was the war cry of the UDA.

THE NUN was shaking my arm, said,

"We're about to land."

My mouth tasted of metal and my eyes hurt, I glanced at
the window, darkness, punctuated by a huge array of lights.
She said,

"They gave us a lovely dinner."

"I'm glad."

Anxiety was sitting in my gut like acid. The wheels hit
the Tarmac and the nun blessed herself. Within fifteen
minutes, the doors were open and passengers began to
move. The nun put out her hand, said,

"A little something as a memento of our trip."

A relic of Padre Pio, she said,

"He's a saint now."

Did you go,

"Yeah, way to go bro . . . or congratulations?"

I said,

"Thank you."

She gave me a look full of what my mother used to call devilment, her eyes dancing,

" 'Tis the oddest thing, you were talking in your sleep."

I waited, fearful of what I might have disclosed and she added,

"You had such a strong Irish accent, isn't that the quarest thing?"

Then she moved into the aisle, said,

"God keep you safe."

I intended buying a gun as backup, lest the Lord didn't hear her.

"You are a foreigner; you do not feel our national animosities as we do."

— GEORGE BERNARD SHAW, *Arms and the Man, Act II*

OUTSIDE THE TERMINAL building, the humidity hit like a hurly. Got my jacket off and loosened the tie, joined the queue for cabs, or as I'd now have to say,

"Got in line."

Moved quickly and then I was in the yellow vehicle, a sense of unreality about it. From hundreds of movies, TV series, the cabs were as familiar as rain. I expected Travis Bickle at the wheel but got a black, wiry guy, asking,

"Where to, dude?"

Told him and we were out of there. Siobhan had booked online, found a place at special rate for ten nights. That was as long as I planned on staying, pick up a piece and head for Tucson, armed and dangerous. The American dream. The hotel was on West Fifty-third, between Fifth and Sixth. I loved just saying the address, it had that short-hand ring, as if you were an old hand. The fare was forty dollars, or forty bucks. Alas, he said dollars, I put ten on top, seemed to do the job. As I got out, I tried,

"Have a good one."

He checked me in the mirror, lazily asked, as if he really couldn't give a fuck,

"You Irish, Bro?"

Shit.

We Irish are supposed to have the lock on hospitality, the warm welcome, all that blarney crap. The Americans have it down pretty tight. At reception, the staff seemed delighted to see me and downright dizzy that I'd chosen to park there. How would I be paying? In Ireland that means cash or charge? Here it was which credit card? Went with American Express.

"Keep it country."

A bellhop carried my bag and he acted like my new best friend. Okay, I could roll with that. Showed me to a large spacious room and I laid a ten on him. E. B. White said you need to be lucky? Better be loaded too. I'd forgotten the whole scam of tipping. Shit, you'd need a second occupation to keep the services running. He told me to have a good evening and I wanted to go,

"Yeah, whatever."

I was getting a headache from the conflict of accents. I unpacked, didn't take long, he who travels light is an ex-army brat.

Then cracked the Bush, poured a large one and took a hefty belt, stood by the window, letting the whiskey warm my stomach.

It did.

Red Rock West, one of my favourite movies, was unreeling in my head, part of my whole fuzzy notion of the West. I finished the drink and dumped the travel clothes in the laundry bag, rang room service, and they pledged to come get them.

Worked for me.

Showered, shaved, did some exercises from my Brit days. Siobhan had given me Aramis, slapped it on, had a *Home Alone* moment as it burned like fuck. Got my address book and picked up the phone, rang a bit then,

"*Sí?*"

"Juan . . . How you doing?"

A moment of silence then,

"Jesús Maria Cristos . . . Stephan . . . is you?"

"None other."

"You are in Nuevo York?"

"Alive and kicking."

"And Thomas, he is with you?"

Alive and kicking seemed now to have been the very worst expression, I said,

"No, he didn't make it."

We arranged to meet at Dino's, a restaurant in the East Village, I asked,

"I don't know it, is it new?"

"*Amigo,* in the village, they're all new."

Juan, Tommy, and I had worked on a building site off Lexington Avenue, upholding the Irish tradition of the *navy.* Our countrymen had built the railways, the roads in the U.K and to hear the Prods tell it, we were now determined to detonate everything we constructed. The pay was amazing and it didn't hurt that the union was Mick. The

Italians might have the rep for the service industry, but we had a solid grasp on the building game. Overtime was the best scam, you stayed an extra ten minutes and they clocked it as like, five hours. How rich is that? Tommy was probably the most unsuitable person for manual work ever, but I covered for him and plus, he had a way with him, people just liked having him around.

After work, we'd go for a few cold ones and Juan began to tag along. He had the best dope I ever smoked. Santa Marta gold, the jackpot for potheads, known as blond, it came from the coast of Colombia, had a distinctive aroma, colour, and gave a high that other pot only imitated. You did a spliff, you were paralysed. I wasn't much taken with dope, I like to stretch my relaxation, slow beers over an evening, conceding control very gradually, settling for a mild buzz.

Tommy loved it, would do a toke first thing in the morning. I'd be making tea and he'd already have a shit-kicking grin in place. I knew he liked to keep a line from reality, would take anything, Valium, booze, ludes, grass, to maintain the barrier against the world, said to me,

"Life sucks."

Mostly I agreed but felt you needed all your faculties to stay afloat. Siobhan had remarked,

"He's the brother you never had."

I'd always thought I looked out for Tommy, walked point to his fragile life. When he'd taken the bullet in the face, my whole charade had nearly come crashing down, a thousand times since I'd muttered,

"You should have seen Stapleton coming."

In granite moments I added,

"Who could have seen him coming?"

I was outside the hotel now, waiting to grab a cab, and the oddest thing, a mangy cat shot out from behind a parked car, dashed across the street, narrowly avoiding being crushed by a van and I swear, before he disappeared into an alley, he paused, looked right at me, then took off.

I felt a shiver down my spine, recalling a story Tommy had told me.

Tommy had brief passions with various things, a book one day, then a movie or a song; for a while, it would be all he could talk about, then just as quickly, he'd drop it, never show the slightest interest again. In Brooklyn he discovered a small bookstore, found a Bukowski and bingo, his new mania. Regaling me morning noon and night with the genius of the guy.

We were in the apartment one night, trying to decide where we'd go for the crack . . . crack being Irish for fun and almost no relation to the drug. I was at the door, ready to roll, Tommy was slugging from a bottle of Miller, reading, I said,

"You're reading now!"

He didn't even look up, said,

"Listen . . . the only battle is to remain as alive as possible."

With more than a little acid in my tone, I said,

"Gee, I'll try to remember that."

He chucked the empty bottle at the waste bin, missed, said,

"Charlie says —"

I interrupted, knowing I was seriously irritating him, asked,

"Whoa, mate, who the hell is Charlie?"

He gave me a look of real hatred,

"Bukowski, haven't you been listening, jeez, Steve, you need to get with the program . . . anyway, he says, anybody can go the way of Dylan Thomas, Ginsberg, Corso, Behan, Leary, Creeley, just sliding down that river of shit, the idea is creation not adulation, the idea is a man in a room alone hacking at a stone and not sucking at the tits of the ground."

We were flush with money, the building site was paying our freight in every way. Tommy hailed a cab, told the driver,

"The Lower East side, let us out at Orchard Street."

I asked him,

"What's with that?"

He grimaced, well fed up with me, said,

"It's where Charlie would head."

When we got out of the cab, we moved onto Delancey Street, and the best I can say about it is, it's a rundown boulevard. I could just about see the Williamsburg Bridge but Tommy ignored that, turned into a dark-looking bar. Being Irish wasn't going to help, the place had an air of hostility, Tommy said,

"Feel the vibe."

It was impossible not to, rife with tension. Tommy ordered a couple of boilermakers and we got a table near the window. I could see the dirty looks we were getting from various guys at the counter. Tommy was oblivious, sank the whiskey, said,

"I could do that."

I was distracted, watching the guys watching us, asked,

"Do what, drink like Bukowski?"

He was quiet and I turned, saw his face, disappointment, hurt, writ large. I tried to rally, asked,

"What's that, seriously, I want to know?"

But he wouldn't be drawn, withdrew into himself, began to drink like . . . Bukowski?

We did a few more rounds and a guy came over, swagger in his eyes, a pool cue in his hand, asked,

"You faggots not talking to each other?"

Tommy was never built for combat, that was my department, if the need arose. He was out of his chair in the blink of an eye, had the guy pinned against the wall, going,

"Do you have a fucking death wish, answer me, you bollix?"

I got him off the guy and we got out of there without any more hassle. I hailed a cab and we got distance and fast, lest they have a change of heart. Tommy was wringing his hands, said,

"I wanted to kill that fucker."

I got him back to the apartment, poured him a large Jameson, our final bottle of duty free, and he began to roll a joint, said,

"I need to chill out."

I had a Miller, always lots of that in the apartment, Tommy bought it by the case from one of the guys on the site. I put on some music, seemed like a Tom Waits moment and Tommy nodded his head as he heard the strangled voice, he smoked the joint, did the last of the Jameson, then hunched over, asked,

"I ever tell you about my cat?"

"What?"

He wasn't listening to me, he was telling this to the void, continued,

"When I was a kid, young, we had a mangy cat, real street urchin, feisty little bastard, fight with anyone, lost an eye in one encounter, didn't stop him, he continued to mix it up."

He looked at me but wasn't really seeing me, said,

"Scrawny little tyke, he loved me, straight up, he'd scratch the bejaysus out of most people, but me, he frigging liked me big-time."

There was wonder in his voice, as if any creature could feel such about him. I wanted to jump in, stayed silent lest I break the mood, he sighed.

"One day, he pawed at the door to get out, I thought he was on his usual patrol, roust the locals. Thing is, he was going to die."

Tommy fixed his eyes on me, asked,

"Did you know that, that they go off alone to die?"

I shook my head.

He peered into his empty glass, stood up to get some brew, said,

"Who cares, right, damn cat, the world is full of them."

An hour or so later, I called it a night and for a while, I could hear him singing along to Tom . . . then finally, he headed for his bed, stood over me for a moment, whispered,

"The thing, the thing I wanted to be . . . is a poet."

I didn't know how to reply and even after all this time, I still don't know. I do know I should have said something.

"I was sitting in a bar on Western Avenue. It was around midnight and I was in my usual confused state. I mean, you know, nothing works right; the women, the jobs, the no jobs, the weather, the dogs. Finally you just sit in a stricken state and wait like you're on the bus stop bench waiting for death.

— CHARLES BUKOWSKI, "No Way to Paradise."

I HAILED A CAB outside the hotel, gave him the address. The driver had a pack of Salems beside his coffee holder, reached over, got one going, *then* asked,

"You care if I smoke?"

No smoking decals were plastered on every available space, I said,

"Knock yourself out."

And got the look. Nice to know some expressions were universal; he must have felt an explanation was necessary, said,

"You're wondering what's with the menthol, am I right?"

I was wondering why he wouldn't shut the fuck up, he said,

"See, I got this, like . . . throat cancer, you know what I'm saying?"

How complex was it? I grunted in a noncommittal way,

you can't encourage them. They're off and running anyway, you show a fraction of interest, they're all over you
like the proverbial bad suit. A statue of the Virgin was on
the dash, with numerous Rosary beads, medals, relics. He
used his cig to indicate the Madonna, asked,

"You know who that is, huh?"

I warranted I didn't and with a triumphant note he said,

"Our Lady of Guadaloupe, she cured my cancer but I
gotta do my bit, you hearing me, you know what I'm
telling you?"

I had the drift.

"So see, I smoke these here menthols, like penance, god
is batting with the triers."

I'd always wanted to ask,

"What about them Knicks?"

But there's not a lot of opportunity in Ireland. Like calling dollars "bucks," we love that stuff. So, I tried it.

He wasn't cranked by my response. A Buick shot out
from behind us, cut right across and rear-ended another
cab. My driver didn't react and I was bitterly disappointed,
I'd wanted him half out of the window, going,

"The fuck's the matter with you, muthahfuckah?"

And such.

Did I want stereotypes, you betcha. I looked out the window, have to write my own script. Steam was rising out of
the manholes, like grey clouds of hope, and I thought,

"That's more like it."

I'd planned on returning to New York for so long, it had
pulled me through many the Irish winter, those Monday
mornings, when dawn breaks at nine and evening sets at

four! Those days that the rain is personal. I'd close my eyes, summon up a New York minute and be comforted. Tommy and I had been here a year, old hands on the site, Tommy was deep into the rip-offs that occur, tools disappearing, materials gone missing, a whole other economy happening. It's lucrative and highly dangerous, you're treading on all sorts of lethal toes. Juan was right along with him, selling to the Mex community who were denied aces to more regular channels.

As usual, I tried to caution him but the edge was where he lived. Juan encouraged his recklessness, driving him to more dangerous stunts. One evening, he helped offload a whole floor of new fittings. I was seriously pissed, ranted,

"You bollix, the hell is the matter with you, you trying to get us killed?"

And got that lopsided grin, like a kid who's been caught with his hand in the till, his reaction a mix of fun and apprehension. He did what he always did when I confronted him, he drank, with intent.

He was your two-fisted drinker, no screwing around. Tommy's father had made me promise a long time ago to look out for Tommy. Like a fool, I promised. My life can be summarised by two conflicting threads: times of near harmony and times of chaos. I veered twixt the two like a nun on a bicycle.

I'd be full of focus, duty, clarity, smarts, if you will, then sheer impulsiveness, a leap into the unknown. When I snap out of the latter, I go scuttling to the former. Can you follow that? It's Irish logic at its most convoluted. I went to college, the only one in generations of pig ignorance. I like music and if you want to follow bands, being a student is the best way to go. Pursue it with a diligence bordering on hysteria. My old man worked on the railways, forty years and got a pocket watch and destroyed lungs. My mother, as Galway as Nora Barnacle and as feisty, would wonder about me, go,

"Where'd we get him?"

If she read, which she didn't, she might have considered Yeats and "The Stolen Child." Would exclaim to her neighbours,

"He's as odd as two left feet."

Because I didn't fit the mold.

Then got the chance to study English at Trinity. Betrayal at the local point. She'd cry,

"We've got a perfectly good University here."

I didn't argue, just forged on, the payoff was that I'd be away from home. The downside was Tommy. Took him for a pint, said,

"They think I shouldn't go to Trinity."

He was in his headbanger phase, speed and Black Sabbath, said,

"Fuck 'em, you gotta go."

I'd been drinking Guinness, the creamy pints before me like communion. Tommy was on cider (Loony juice), his third, with Jack Daniels chasers, I'd reached the crux, said,

"What about you, buddy?"

He raised his glass, clinked mine, said,

"Me? I'm going with."

And did.

Changed his act, at least outwardly, got a job in a bookies and began the highs and lows that marked his life.

Money.

He'd amass it, blow it, in/out, punctuated with dope. The booze, regular and habitual as it was, was support to the main event. He'd read, no, studied *Fear and Loathing In Las Vegas* and became a Gonzo convert. He financed the college years. We drank in Mulligan's and the Joyce connection was never mentioned. After my degree, I felt I'd gone soft. Dublin was terrific but the years of booze, fish and chips suppers, blew my gut out. I hated that, saw it as weakness, loss of control. That, I dread above all. Over one too many Jamesons, at some club in Leeson Street, I said to Tommy,

"Man, I've got to get in shape."

He was downing Tequila slammers, said,

"Join the army."

"Okay."

Clink of glasses, then I asked,

"What about you?"

"Me? I'll come with."

Did.

Second betrayal, the worst an Irishman can do, joined the British army. They kicked the fuck out of me. Stationed on the Salisbury Plains, as dead a place as you envisage; if Irish rain is, as they say, *soft*, then the stuff in the UK is as cold as the pubs during Lent.

Tommy was managing a bookies in Salisbury, up to his arse in dope, scams, and risk. Three months in, I was in bad shape. We were downing pints of bitter, JD chasers.

One of the very rare nights I'd off, he said,

"Jack it."

"What?"

"Throw in the towel, leg it, what the fuck do you care?"

I cared.

Two points heavily against me in the army, I was Irish and maybe worse, a college boy.

Fuck on a blackboard.

A double header of destruction. They were trying to kill me and not even being subtle about it. My front teeth had been knocked out, the new crowns hurting like a son of a bitch. I downed the JD, said,

"I signed on for a year, I'll do the year."

Tommy signalled another round, ensuring prompt service with,

"And whatever you're having yourself."

Gave me one of his rare looks of total openness, he had the eyes of a child, said,

"My money's on you, Steve-o."

I managed to last the full twelve months in the army, it was as vicious and brutal as I could have imagined. Eight months in, the sergeant said to me,

"You want to try for the stripes?"

He hadn't called me Paddy, which they did at every opportunity and that made me cautious. I asked,

"What stripes?"

"Corporal."

I never hesitated, said

"No . . . thanks."

He had begun by loathing me, trying every which way to break me, and slowly, he'd begun to ease up as I completed each task. I was in shape, and a confidence had crept in as I realised I had an aptitude for the life. He stared at me, said

"Don't be a thick, Paddy, it's a chance to move up, lots of perks, plus, you get to give orders."

I held his stare, he no longer scared me, asked,

"And the men, they're going to take orders from a . . . Paddy?"

He spat on the ground, one of his less endearing habits, said,

"You make them follow orders, that's why it's called command."

I didn't bite. I'd found a niche, a way of keeping my head down, watching my back and staying alive, I'd saved most of my pay, and knew I could get through. The sergeant was disgusted and stomped off.

One of the squaddies, guy named Sheils, from up North, had been on my case from day one. Always with the Irish jokes, the stealing of my gear, screwing with my head. He hated the Irish, liked to say,

"I'm of Scots Protestant descent and we colonised your godforsaken country, what we'd get? Fucking bombs in our public toilets, shot in the back. . . ."

He had the truly dangerous blend of arrogance and stupidity, he'd have been seriously threatening if he'd one ounce of intelligence. I'd learned a vital lesson from the Brits, take your time. So I bit down, and with every successive humiliation, like urine in my bed, glass in my porridge, I acted like it was no biggie.

Sitting in the pub in Salisbury with Tommy, my first Saturday off in weeks, I told him about Sheils. Tommy was flush, he was making money hand over fist and spending at an equal rate. He was drinking gin, said,

"You ask the fuck for Jameson, he says, they don't stock Mick piss."

That kind of place.

Tommy could care less, the insults of the world he didn't take personally anymore, he'd been so severely hurt for so long, he just assimilated it into the whole bleak view he maintained. I was drinking pints of bitter and well-named it was. I daren't lose control, my life literally depended on it.

Tommy asked,

"You have rifles, yeah?"

"Course."

"With live ammunition?"

"Sure."

"Shoot the bollix."

He reached in his jacket, took out a packet, said,

"Got you something."

This was a first, we didn't do gifts, wasn't sure what to say so I said nothing, unwrapped it. A black leather wallet, with a crest on the front. A shield with a diamond in the centre, crisscrossed with two heavy lines and on the top, a cat . . . a fiery looking animal but a cat nevertheless. A logo beneath in Latin, roughly translated as virtue and nobility.

It was the Blake coat of arms, my family name. I said,

"Jesus, I didn't even know we had a crest, let alone a motto, how'd you find that?"

He was smiling, a real smile, not his usual cynical one, said,

"The Internet."

I said,

"I'm delighted, thanks."

He waved it off, said,

"You Prods, you like yer coat of arms."

I kept it light, said,

"We haven't been Protestant for donkey's years."

He was looking for the barman, said,

"Ah, once a Prod, always a Prod, you check in there, there's a secret compartment."

But we got distracted and I never did get to find the secret pocket.

The other lesson I'd learned in Salisbury was to fight dirty. None of that gentleman crap. You fought by the rules and they handed you your arse. Eventually, Sheils got tired ragging me, he'd still make the odd gesture, spit in my coffee, but he'd lost the momentum. Early morning, in the washroom, he was shaving, whistling the theme from *The Bridge on the River Kwai*. I locked the door, picked up the metal waste bucket and blindsided him. The force of the blow actually dented the metal. I caught him before he fell, asked,

"You hear about the Paddy who goes into a bathroom..."

Then gave him the kidney punches we'd been taught ... continuing

"Says to an English guy ..."

I got him into the stall, put his head in the bowl.

"What's the difference between a horse and an Englishman?"

Pulled his head up, butted him between the eyes, then broke his nose.

"You can bet on a horse."

I don't think he found it very funny, but then, Irish jokes are a lot of things, funny is rarely one of them.

A LONG TIME after the principal players in this story were
buried, I was sitting one cold February evening in New
York, in a studio apartment in the West Village, watching
the snow fall, a full-on melancholy building. The windchill
factor was ferocious, a neighbour, the only one who spoke
to me, said,

"I'm not venturing out till late May."

Got my vote.

I had a glass of Jameson in my right hand, The Water-
boys on the speakers. A group founded by a guy from Edin-
burgh, Mike Scott, they ended up in Galway, laid down a
couple of classic tracks and made little impact outside of
Ireland. At the time when U2 was about to conquer America, the boys were playing small venues in Ireland. Their
following may have been small in rock terms but it was
fierce in its enduring loyalty. "The Whole of the Moon"
was spinning and if I had to describe my love for Siobhan,

the difference between us, their lyrics may best capture it, saying:

"I saw the crescent, you she saw the whole of the moon."

Did she ever.

A time when she had a semi-nervous breakdown, I think she was seventeen or so and she saw a head doctor, as they call them in Ireland. She told me that he said,

"You are quite unique in that you have no illusions and that is a hard way to live."

Jesus, to see to the granite core of the world, I couldn't hack it like that. I have to believe in . . . shit, I dunno, some kind of hope. Siobhan believed you made your own luck, and thanks to me, she ran out of all the hard-earned luck she'd strived so long to achieve and that is my burden. It's not so much that I led her astray but that I had her think a new life was not only possible but within reach. She'd done all the work, and me, I let it unravel. They say no sin is unforgivable, well, they're wrong. I believe there is one sin without redemption and that is to hold out the prospect of a better life and through sheer fecklessness, to let it slip away. If the Jesuits are correct and the fires of hell are being stoked for me, I'm going to ask,

"Put on a few more coals."

"But to be American is to be Nietzschean in half of
yourself. You move beyond sin even if part of you
still believes in it."

— HAROLD BRODKEY, *This Wild Darkness:*
The Story of My Death

STEVE-O.

Tommy's term of affection for me.

An old joke, combining *Hawaii Five–O* and care. After
the army, we moved back to Galway, I tried teaching but
couldn't hack the normality. It was to Tommy, on one of
those endless winter evenings, when it's raining, cold,
dark, fucking primeval, I proposed,

"Let's go to America."

In jig time, we were in New York. I got on the building
site straightaway but Tommy joined Kinney's, the cleaning
contractors, and ended up scraping chewing gum from the
floor of Radio City; he couldn't believe such a job existed
and it nearly killed him, he said,

"You cannot imagine how difficult it is to get that shit
off a carpet, and man, the places they stick it."

So I put in the word and he got to join me at the site.
We'd a year of wild and wildest abandon.

*   *   *

The cab stopped and the driver intoned,

"Dino's, that like new?"

"You're asking me?"

He was already on a different track, fiddling with the radio, heard the sports, hit the dash, shouted,

"Goddamn Jets choked."

I paid the freight and laid a five on top, then on impulse, added the nun's Padre Pio, he said,

"Caramba, He is the man."

Then, as he placed the relic beside yhe Virgin, added,

"Watch your ass."

He was already firing up another menthol as he burned rubber outta there. The Madonna had her work cut out, is how I figured it. I took a moment on the sidewalk, what we call footpaths. Get my face in gear. Truth was, Juan was an arsehole but Tommy rated him, so, so I'd gone along. They had dope in common. I never quite figured if Juan was Mexican, Puerto Rican but he affected characteristics of each and was big on the macho bullshit.

I opened the door of the place and stepped in. A bar ran along one wall and then ten to fifteen tables scattered around. Right down at the end was Juan and not alone, a blond woman beside him. He raised his arm

"Stephan, *amigo, hombre.*"

His lean on my name was a pain but I let it slide, walked to greet him, already regretting I'd made the call. He moved, threw his arms round me, intense hug, going,

"*Muy bueno, muchacho.*"

I think.

Some Spanish shit anyway. Over his shoulder, my eyes locked with the woman. And wallop, my heart did a jig, as fast and unexpected as that. A very pretty face, like Virginia Madsen in her early twenties. It was the look in her eyes that snared me, consisting of ... amusement, heat, smirk.

As if she'd known me and knew exactly what I was thinking. I was thinking I'd sell my soul to have her, Jesus. It came totally out of left field, I loved Siobhan with every fibre of my being, she was the love that *passes all understanding*. I just couldn't imagine life without her. This heat, this . . . I hate to admit it, this pure lust was something I'd never experienced. And didn't want.

Juan finally released me, stood back, said

"*Hombre*, you look good."

He was wearing a loose shirt, bright red over white combat pants, boots, very worn, very scruffed. The stacked heels brought him to my chin. His skin was sallow and he had a soft face, almost feminine till you saw the eyes, something lurked there, cautioned you to move with extreme care. When he hugged me, at the base of his spine I felt the outline of the gun. Weapons were always a feature with him. I guessed him to be my age, a year off forty, yet when he smiled, which was often, he could pass for early twenties. The smile had never been connected to warmth, he extended his hand, went,

"*Amigo*, meet my ol' lady, Sherry. Babe, get your ass up, meet my soul bro."

Dolly Parton memorably said,

"You know how much it costs to look this cheap?"

Sherry had the same idea. About five feet five and all of it trouble. Wearing a tight black halter neck that barely contained her breasts, it didn't so much cling as hang on for dear life and who wouldn't? A short black skirt of some shiny material that I swear glistened. Sheer black nylons that couldn't be hose, too goddamm sexy and the "come get me" heels. My breath was caught in my chest, Juan said,

"Go woman, give him a big one."

Yeah.

There was a mocking tone in his voice, he knew the effect. She leaned over, kissed me on both cheeks, the aroma of her perfume was dizzying. Beneath it, something else, raw sexuality. She whispered,

"Poison."

Then moved back, gave me that smile, said,

"The perfume."

Juan clapped me on the back, said,

"I'll get us some drinks, yes?"

He moved along to a swarthy guy in an Armani suit and they began an intense conversation. I sat opposite Sherry, she had a pack of Virginia Slims, slid one out, put it in her mouth, waited. I picked up a book of matches, struck one, leaned over, a slight tremor in my fingers, she cupped my hand, said,

"Easy."

Caution or encouragement?

She blew a perfect ring, watched it curl above us, like an omen of very bad karma. Her accent had hooked me, it was trailer trash with a hint of hillbilly and a hard nasal underlay to edge it along. I asked, like I gave a toss,

"Isn't it illegal to smoke here?"

Now she let her whole face smile, from her eyes to her even small perfect teeth, said,

"If it's fun, it's illegal, yeah?"

Argue that.

I said,

"You're not a New Yorker."

The question irritated her, saw it wipe the smile from her eyes, as if she expected more, better, she said,

"Yo, bud, newsflash: Ain't nobody from New York, I'm from Tallahassee."

She lingered on the name, drawing it out then rising on the last syllable, I said,

"Like the song?"

Blank look, then,

"Song?"

"Sure. Bobby Gentry, Billy Joe McAllister jumped off that bridge."

Didn't register, she indicated her empty glass, said,

"We drinking, or what?"

I looked round and Juan had disappeared, she said,

"He's got a jones."

My turn to blank, so she sighed, made the gesture of a needle into a vein. I noticed her nails, black polish. Should have been ugly but worked. 'Course, I was already sold and would have appreciated any shade. Juan had always been into dope, him and Tommy, bags of grass, moving up or down to coke. I was riveted by her eyes, flecks of green in there, I asked,

"How serious is his habit?"

More derision, as if she couldn't quite get how dumb I was, dissed,

"You're shooting up, how the fuck serious does it get?"

The obscenity hung in the air, like a bad news flash, to ease it, I stood, asked,

"Wine, right?"

She nodded, stared at me, said,

"Nice buns."

Threw me, I countered,

"The Girl with Green Eyes."

Blank again so I explained,

"It's a novel, by an Irish writer, Edna O'Brien, she . . ."

Her hand was up, said,

"Like the wine? Before Tuesday."

An Italian guy at the till, I asked,

"Bottle of wine."

He looked past me, at Sherry, said,

"Bottles."

Handed me two, another glass and I headed back, I'd been tempted to ask if he'd seen Juan but if he'd gone,

"Juan who?"

I'd have decked him. Jet lag, new city, Juan, had combined to make my headache start up again. When I sat down, it must showed as Sherry asked,

"You hurting?"

The "hurting" made it sound like a country song, I said,

"The miles catching up."

She held my gaze, then,

"Got some ludes, fix you right up."

I poured the wine, said,

"I'm not real gone on dope."

She took her glass, said,

"Juan said you were a tight ass."

Showstopper.

Then I felt her toes touch my left thigh, a light caress then withdrew, said,

"Juan catches you messing with me, he'll put a cap in your skull."

"What?"

"We're married, yeah, so you know what you're getting into big guy."

She was insane, no doubt about it, she was your out-and-out lunatic. I figured I'd give it five minutes, then get the hell out of there. I'd fulfilled my obligation to Tommy, met Juan and that was it, deal done.

Juan returned, an energy burning off him, you could almost reach out and touch it, a manic fire. He said,

"More vino, *bueno*."

Whatever his origins, Juan dived in and out of accents like a demented seal. When he was high, which was most of the time, he'd spin from Spanish to English to Pidgin at a blistering pace. My headache moved up a notch. I poured him a glass and he said,

"To Tommy, *mi amigo*."

We clinked glasses and he drained his. Dopers, they're cruising on some junk, they'll take whatever else is to hand, especially your cash. Tommy telling me one time, you go a cokehead's apartment, the first thing you see is tons of dry cleaning, all on hangers, in cellophane, ready to rock. No waiting. Juan asked,

"*Qué passé* Stephan, where is Thomas?"

I looked at them, two hyped strangers, my head pounding, said,

"He's dead."

Sherry was filing her nails and for a moment, Juan sat absolutely still then grabbed my wrist, demanded,

"What is this . . . this sheet?"

I stared at his fingers, the nails bitten to the quick, said,

"You want to let go of my wrist...*amigo?*"

He released it, sat back and I said,

"He didn't suffer."

What a crock that is, as if it gives some sort of closure. A bleakness filled Juan's face then his eyes were hardass, asked,

"How?"

"An accident."

He began flexing his fingers, cracking the joints, Sherry said,

"Yo, guys, lighten up."

Without looking at her, he said,

"Shut up, bitch."

Then to me,

"You are his friend, you watch his back, how can he *muerto*, dead?"

I could do hardass, welcomed it; he pushed, I'd push back, said,

"Shit happens."

Just like that, he let it go, shrugged, made the sign of the cross, asked,

"Tell me your plans, *amigo?*"

Had fully intended laying out my Tucson project, meeting him now, I way backtracked, lied,

"Thought I'd hang out, you know, like chill."

Before he could respond, his cell trilled, he flipped it open with such casualness, I knew he'd practiced it a hundred times in the mirror, went,

"*Diga* me."

Listened, then followed with a volley of spitfire Spanish,

chewing the words in a flurry of facial grimaces I could only half understand. Went like this:

"*Dinero, mucho dinero, trabajo, carambe, muy bueno.*"

And a litany of obscenities. Slammed the phone on the table, shouting,

"*Maricón.*"

His eyes were crazed and he jumped to his feet, said,

"*Amigo*, gotta vamoose, some business to fix."

He pronounced it *bidness*. I said,

"No problem."

He indicated Sherry, not looking at her, asked,

"Can you see my woman gets home, maybe catch a cab?"

And he rooted in his skin tight-jeans, spilled a mess of bills on the table, said,

"We hook up *mañana*, have us a time."

He was reaching out to make that black gesture, knuckles touching, then palms over and more cool shit, I ignored it, said,

"You bet."

We all looked at his palm dangling in mid air then he recovered, leaned over to Sherry, got his tongue half way down her throat. Took a time as he made slavering noises, as if he were eating her, then withdrew, made a gun of his finger, cocked the thumb, said,

"See you, slick."

After he'd gone, I said,

"Bidness?"

She was applying lipstick, a shiny pale gloss, said,

"Thinks he's a player, grew up in the goddamn Bronx."

"And is he . . . a player?"

She adjusted her skirt, not that there was a whole lot to fix, but gave us both the opportunity to stare at her legs, then she said,

"He's a goddamn prick is what he is."

No argument there.

"Sherry is what Connemara men drink when they give up booze for Lent, they feel it's a true penance."

— TRADITIONAL

SHERRY WAS BORN as Mary Ellen Dubcheck in the type of mining town made famous by *The Deer Hunter*. When she finally saw the movie, she was convinced, first, they'd made it in her hometown, and second, she thought Christopher Walken was the hottest guy on the planet.

The term dysfunctional is too mild for the family she had — seriously fucked is closer. Her father was a shadowy figure who beat her, then just upped and disappeared. Laying the seeds of abandonment rage in the young girl, for the rest of her life she'd be acutely aware of men attempting to leave her. Her mother was the trailer trash of Gretchen Wilson songs, the proverbial redneck woman.

What Sherry remembered of her town was the thick pallor of grit, dust, black smoke that hung over the landscape like the worst omen. It got in your eyes, hair, clothes, and no amount of scrubbing would erase it. When the steelworks were closed, a blacker depression settled on the place. The men, drank, fought and hunted. The atmosphere was rife with hurt, hatred, resentment, and all of it laid its curse on the girl.

One brother, Lee, a year older, interfered with her when she was twelve, and when she told her mother, she got the beating of a lifetime with the words,

"It's what men do, stop whining or there's more whipping. . . ."

Lee was found dead from a gunshot wound to the back of the head in the woods. Hunting accident they said. Sherry's mother thought otherwise but said nothing. Their dog, a collie named Rusty, was also the victim of a *hunting accident.* Rusty had hated the young girl with the unerring instinct that canines have for the very essence of malevolence. Her mother packed Sherry off to New Orleans when the girl was fourteen. To a friend who ran a whorehouse. Sherry learned all she needed to know for survival, sex equals power equals violence. A combination of that trinity would run her life from then on. Having been schooled in the very essentials of survival and manipulation, Sherry lit out for New York when she was seventeen. Arriving at Port Authority, like the thousands of runaways and prey who arrive daily, she was hit on by one of the waiting friendly predators. He sure dialled the wrong number. His usual gig being to get the girl to a house, then turn her out to a line of men. In a New Orleans drawl, Sherry asked if he'd like a little suck before they left the station?

They found him in the urinal, his pants around his ankles and his dick in his mouth, a cathouse variation on the blow job, his wallet missing.

Sherry got a job as a dancer in the East Village and pulled

down the bucks with a wild routine that involved an imaginary dog she called Rusty and sometimes, for private customers, she called the dog Lee.

How she hooked up with Juan, she spotted his thick wedge of green from the stage and within a week, he'd set her up in a cosy studio. His use of heroin meant the sex was sporadic but he kept her around as she was so sharp. Called her his private dancer. Sherry loved the big city, she got her own supply of drugs set up and had plenty of green. She sent her mother a fat package with half a Ben Franklin and the words,

"I left the other half in the woods, like men do."

Juan had offered her some crank but she was too slick to go that road, she had a nice buzz on a daily basis from the dope she'd been reared on in New Orleans — Percodan — she dearly loved her percs. Mix in a little crystal for variation and a girl was as happy as a pig in a basket. She worked on her accent, learning to vary it with down home licks and the harsh vowels of the Lower East Side.

Scams . . .

Nothing she liked better than a good one. *House of Games* was her favourite movie, with the line, "one born every minute and two to take 'em." She stumbled into a rich seam almost by accident.

Forty-second Street, cleaned up and tourist attraction though it still had enough sleaze to make her feel comfortable. And if you hung out close to Port Authority, she saw most of them go down. It was a master class in the con. Became her custom to take her latte, grande, with vanilla lick, in the Starbucks on the corner opposite. Plus, one of the geeks, calling himself a *barista*, had the hots for her and threw in a Danish free. Turned out the nerd had a little habit going and so she established another minor connection for her medication, never could have enough sources. Juan, though not stingy with his dope, sometimes threatened to cut her off, keep her in line, the usual macho bullshit.

She was ripping him off daily but a little at a time. Never knew when the time might come , she'd have to leg it and best be prepared. A cold Monday, the windchill howling down Sixth Avenue, she made her way to the coffee stop, got her smile and latte, took her usual seat near the restrooms. The cold ensured the place was jammed and a business type asked if he might share her table. In his forties, he had the hairline of the harassed executive. He put his briefcase on the table, then supped loudly on his cardboard cup. Sherry got her best smile in place, the one she'd rehearsed a hundred times, a hint of timidity, a dribble of heat and a whole lot of promise. Never failed. She flashed it, said,

"Lemme guess, mocha with a dash of peppermint."

She'd heard him order the damn thing. He was amazed and lured by the smile, went,

"Well, good Lord, that is astonishing."

Yeah, right.

He was wearing a red string on his wrist, beneath a Rolex.

He caught her look, used his fingers to touch the band, said,

"The Kabbalah, it protects from the evil eye."

She nearly laughed, thinking, you're going to need more than a piece of string to protect you now buddy. She put on her most *oh please educate me kind sir* expression, asked,

"What's that about?"

He explained that he suffered from recurring anxiety/depression woes then heard about Philip Berg, the founder of The Kabbalah Centre, and his life had been changed. He named Madonna and Britney Spears as two devotees. If he thought this would convince Sherry, he couldn't have chosen worse names. Sherry thought these dames were seriously whacko. Her only heroine was Roseanne Barr, badass and rich.

She near simpered,

"And have you met Madonna, Guy . . . and oh, their divine little girl, Lourdes?"

He wasn't pleased as it distracted him from the main topic, himself. She quickly got that rectified by asking,

"How do I get one of those . . . bands?"

She was careful not to call it string. He patiently outlined that she could attend The Kabbalah Centre, purchase the item for twenty-six dollars and the book of learning was only three hundred or so. He offered to take her. Within a few hours, she'd taken him for his wallet, the Rolex, and on a whim, took the red band, too. Left him on a bed in the Milford Plaza. As she headed towards Penn Station, a homeless guy asked her for help, she gave him the string, and he whined,

"The fuck is that?"

She gave her sweetest smile, said,

"The answer to your recurring anxiety *slash* . . .

She emphasised the slash, leaning on it, getting some heat in there, then,

". . . depression, problems lie in that little piece of magic."

She had Juan buy her a laptop, well, he acquired one, paying for things wasn't his territory and she looked up cults, got her a list of religious groups, including, the Brethren, Sai Ba, Jews For Jesus, Raelians, Beta Domination. Over the next few months she met and rolled representatives of most of these.

Her database also turned up Aryan Nations, Satanic Church, and web addresses such as www.godhatesfags. com. The tone of these folk reflected her own personality too much for her to fuck with them; she knew they weren't the ones to go after as they'd come right back and with ferocity. Like everything else, she grew bored with the whole deal, she couldn't face one more earnest-faced, veggie, non-caffeinated, positive do-gooder.

Sherry liked to walk. New York was full of wonders, every trip out was an adventure. A brisk march day, Juan had took off to conduct some *bidness* in Chicago, Sherry was walking along Christopher Street, she'd heard one of the crew mention that from Sheridan Square down to the Hudson was the territory of the *maricón*, the gay enclave. On West Street she watched in wonder as openly gay couples walked hand-in-hand. She walked on to Grove Street, saw a café called Marie's Crisis Café, and went in. Ordered a large latte with vanilla, slice of Danish. She wouldn't be eating it but liked the possibility.

Sherry only ever admired one human being, Roseanne Barr, had never missed her show.

Roseanne was true grit, had balls like no else on the planet, stuck it to everyone and now had the fuck-you money that Sherry wanted. A woman sat at her table, asked,

"Join you, hon?"

She was in her fifties but cosmetic surgery had worked its limited miracle. Her neck was old but her face was that of a twenty-year-old. Sherry said,

"You're sitting so I'd say you've already joined me."

The woman laughed, then launched into a very explicit account of her female lovers, followed by a long tirade about the failings of men. Sherry waited till she ran down then used one of Roseanne's lines,

"Why're you complaining, you don't have to fuck them?"

Got her attention real fast.

She invited Sherry back to her place for a drink, some *relaxation*. Sherry said she'd love that.

The apartment was small but tastefully decorated, she produced a bottle of Grey Goose vodka, asked,

"This to your liking, hon?"

Sherry smiled, asked to see the bottle, the woman going,

"It's a good one."

And handed over the bottle. Sherry hefted it in one hand then swung it fast, splitting the woman's forehead like an egg, swung twice more before the woman was out. Sherry took the cap off the bottle, swigged and said,

"It *is* good."

She kicked the woman in the back of the head, going,

"Goddamn dyke."

The apartment yielded an ounce of grass, nearly three hundred bucks, a soft leather jacket that fit perfectly, and some decent-quality earrings.

Later, she was having a drink in The Monster, on Sheridan Square itself, she asked the bartender about the pedestrian walkway that links Battery Park to the top of the Village.

The bartender said that it was fine during the day, packed with bladers, bikers, joggers, but at night, the predators came out. Sherry adjusting the collar of her new soft leather, said,

"You mean it's dangerous?"

Giving her wide eyed look.

The bartender shook his head, said,

"Bitty thing like you, they'd eat you up."

The first thing people were aware of when meeting Sherry was the raw sexuality, it oozed from her. A palpable heat that seemed to shimmer in her aura. She knew and worked it every way she could. Not till afterwards, when you'd gotten away from her, did another sense hit.

An icy cold.

James Hillman, a Jungian psychotherapist, named icy coldness as one of the prime features of evil.

Sherry was able to hide that when you first met her, such was her sensuality that it cloaked the ice. It was literally only when you were away from the fire did the cold set in. Her mother had said,

"You walk into a room, you feel the cold, you know *she* has been here."

Sherry was never referred to by name by her mother, who said,

"I'm scared to say that demon's name."

Juan, who spent more time with Sherry than anyone, was not immune to the sensation, but being on heroin, he put it down to the smack.

The lesbian who'd picked her up in the coffee bar, recuperating in the hospital, would only ever say afterwards,

"I'm so cold, why can't I get warm."

The old people in Ireland, you ever ask them about Satan, about the fires of hell, they'd utter, as they made the sign of the cross,

" 'Tis not the heat you need to concern yourself about, 'tis the cold."

Ask them to elaborate and they'd go,

"Pray to God you never find out."

Juan was getting dangerously out of control, the junk he was shooting was making him meaner than he was by nature and she saw an example of how quickly he could turn. One of his most trusted crew, a stoner named Max, had been with Juan for years. Max had a thing for Sherry, as did most of the crew. He made the mistake of letting it show. A Saturday night, they'd been to a club in Tribeca, Juan liked to think the upper echelons accepted him, they accepted his dope. Max had a few brewskis going, asked Sherry to dance, she looked at Juan who smiled, said,

"Sure, *hermano.*"

Max, downing a triple martini, got her in a clinch on the floor, let his hands fondle her ass. Over his shoulder, she could see Juan, his face like a corpse. It got her hot. She whispered in Max's ear,

"Bet you make all the girls want more."

Max, the poor schmuck, had enough brew in him to call her *puta*, making it like a term of reckless endearment. There is never enough booze in your guts to call a woman like Sherry a whore, in any language, and the endearment hasn't been coined to sugarcoat it. To her, it would always be a lash in the face and required blood — yours. Max was about to add,

"The *mamacitas*, they like to eat the meat, they get some Max, ain't no other *hombre* gonna do."

He never got to utter this sweet nothing as his face was stinging and his head felt like he'd been walloped. He had. Sherry had stepped back, her Jimmy Choos near slipping from her feet, and she swung with her right fist, knocking, if not sense, at least a whole new focus into him. Then she was stomping back to the table, she saw a tiny smile reach Juan's mouth. She had scored on two fronts, made Juan happy and got to fuck with Max.

Any other bitch, Max would have cut her right then, reached for the knife in his boot, but he caught himself, she was the woman of his *patron*. He slouched, like the beast towards Bethlehem, to his boss's table, expecting Armageddon. Juan was laughing, asked,

"*Mi amigo*, you upset my *mariposa, qué?*"

Qué . . . the question posed in Spanish, the echoes of Khe San were what reverberated in the tone. Max launched into a litany of profuse apologies, calling on the Madonna, Her Son, and any other saint that came to mind. Juan waved it off, went,

"No biggie, *mi amigo*, we drink, we fool around, no *problema*, is true?"

Max hoped to fuck it was. Sherry gave him a wicked smile and he got his hopes up all over again that maybe he might be putting the meat to her. More drinks came and an air of festivity resumed, Juan paid particular attention to Max, recalling all their past glories. Then, Juan said they'd move on, he needed to collect some merchandise from his warehouse.

It was a basement off Bleeker Street. Apart from Max, Sherry, Juan, they were accompanied by Ramon, the designated driver, and two new guys from Rosario, lowlifes who crossed the border and were recent additions to the Juan posse, they were supposedly distant relations of his mother's. In the limo, Juan had Max in the back and shared some lines of coke with him, all the time cheering him as his main *hombre*. Sherry, on the other side of Juan, felt her blood sing as she knew there was going to be something medieval. When Juan was this elated, it always ended in gore.

Laughing, and high-fiving, the crew piled into the basement. It was packed with designer gear from the five boroughs. Juan was an equal opportunity thief, taking from every direction. Centre piece was a long, wooden table, old and gnarled. Cases of booze lined the floor. Juan said,

"Yo bro, mix up a batch of margaritas, we gonna get down."

Max was looking for the tequila when Juan blindsided him with a baseball bat. He regained consciousness, his head on fire, and found himself tied to a chair, his hands extended on the table, fastened tight. A loud blast of salsa was roaring in his ears. Seated across from him was Sherry, sipping a margarita. She winked. Juan was flexing a mean-looking cleaver, saying,

"Piece of Taiwan shit, ees no sharp."

He'd lapsed into Mex-speak, a sure sign he had lost it in more ways than in speech pattern. He sunk the cleaver into the table, close to Max's arm, asked,

"What you think, *mi compadre*, ees gonna do the *trabajo*?"

Max tried to speak but sheer terror seemed to have frozen his throat. Juan pulled the cleaver out, asked,

"You like to use your *manos* to pat my *mariposa*'s butt? That what you like, you call her *puta* . . . eh, *maricón*?"

Max stared at Sherry, his eyes, wild in his head, imploring her for intercession, she smiled demurely, raised her glass. Juan moved in close, asked,

"Which *mano* you want to lose, which one you use to wipe your asshole, you choose, left or right?"

Then brought the cleaver down, half severing the right arm, shouted,

"Ah, *caramba*."

The guys from Rosario took a few swings and though it took a good twenty minutes, they finally removed both arms. Juan, sweat rolling down his face, took the limbs, tossed them on the table, said,

"You a hands-on kind of guy, eh, *muchacho*?"

The hands they threw in a Dumpster, get a rise out of the sanitation guys, and Max, Max went into the East River. Ramon, who'd been silent all evening, finally asked,

"How he going to swim, no arms."

That cracked them all up.

Sherry kept that blunt cleaver at the forefront of her mind. The same evening, Juan actually went to bed with her, not that it took long, tops three minutes and she'd learnt all she needed in New Orleans about groaning and urging . . . *go, you stallion*. It never ceased to amaze her the crap that men believed, you made orgasmic noises and they truly accepted they were the hottest lover this side of the Rockies. Juan, well into the junk, barely got thirty seconds of effort into the act, she faked the other two minutes, thirty seconds. Sure, she timed him, she'd little else to do while he grunted like a hog in stew.

One of her fantasies was to hold a mirror up to a guy as he heaved and blew, let him see what she had to see, it might put them off the fierce bullshit they peddled.

Juan had fallen back, exhausted, she lit a Camel, unfiltered, 'cos he was so macho, put it in his mean mouth, cooed,

"You make me so wet."

She knew he was already thinking of his next hit of horse, then he looked at her, asked,

"You ever think, you like to do it with some other *hombre?*"

She made all the right noises, he was the best, the *mega*, satisfied her like no other could, and other dreary garbage. She kept a blade on her side of the mattress, for the day he turned, as turn he surely would. Then she'd gut him like the reptile he was.

Meantime, she fantasized about some dream lover who'd take her the hell away from all this shit.

On a junket to Vegas, she'd persuaded Juan to bring her along, he wasn't hot on the idea, had his crew and obviously had planned on a guys' tour of Vegas. She loaded him up on ludes, got those margaritas into him, and dragged his sorry ass to the Little White Chapel, got hitched.

Juan wasn't real happy about it the next day but shrugged, he had a method of divorce that was indeed final if push came to shove, so he thought, *Let it ride . . . for now.*

"Get away from her, you bitch!"

— RIPLEY, *Aliens*

SHERRY'S HEAD was lying on my chest, her hand on my balls; she said,

"I think you're ready to go again."

I moved her hand, pulled myself upright, got the pillow against my back and remembered I'd asked myself in the cab,

"What's the dumbest, the most reckless thing you can do, what would be like, *the worst idea?*"

I'd just done it. Sherry sat up, reached for her cigs, got one cranked. I couldn't believe what I said:

"This is a non-smoking room."

She asked,

"Yeah, where's the non-fucking room?"

Then she blew smoke at the ceiling, said,

"So fuck 'em, let 'em come get me . . ."

She flicked the ash on the floor, saw me looking, shrugged, then,

"Juan finds you fucked me, he'll kill you."

I caught her wrist, said,

"Enough with the tough-broad routine, okay, it's like tired . . . and could you stop, you know, calling what we did . . . calling it . . . am . . ."

She was amused, said,

"Isn't that kinda cute, you want it to be special, how'd you like me to say it, lovemaking, that make you swoon?"

I got out of bed, pulled on boxers, T-shirt, and went to get some water. On the table was a brochure for Tucson, even the motel we planned on, the aptly named Lazy 8, and various guides to Arizona, all concentrating on a lengthy stay. Last night, hot to trot, full of bad wine, it never occurred to me to put them away. Thinking with my dick. Checked my watch, six in the morning, and Sherry reading my mind, said,

"You're wondering what Juan is thinking, like where the fuck his wife is at?"

Might as well fess up, said,

"It crossed my mind."

She was out of bed, pulling on clothes, said,

"He'll be wasted, he won't surface till noon, then he'll come home."

I said,

"Handy arrangement."

And she shouted,

"Don't get judgemental, hotshot, you've no idea how my marriage is, you met me eight hours ago, you jumped my bones, and now you . . . like . . . know me?"

Before I could apologise, admit I was outta line, she completely changed. The rage evaporated in a moment and now she was almost perky, indicated the brochures, asked,

"Want me to tag along, touch you in Tucson?"

Something in the way she used *touch*, an almost imperceptible hiss, gave me pause, then I said,

"It was just a notion, I've got brochures for all sorts of places."

She was hiking up her skirt, her breasts on display, asked,

"Let's see 'em?"

"What?"

"The other brochures, let's see 'em."

Fuck.

I waved it off, tried,

"Don't you want to shower, get freshened up while I brew some coffee?"

She pulled on her top, the one that had shone in the light last night, didn't glisten much now, her head was down, her voice real low with,

"I want to see the other brochures."

I headed for the bathroom, maybe when I finished, she'd be gone, like Bob Dylan's "Waiting on a Miracle."

Asked myself,

"The fuck I'm doing, having a shower this time of the morning?"

Got in there, shut the door, nearly locked it, had to fight the impulse; shaved, taking it slow, killing time. Had the shower to scalding, burn off the paranoia. Finally emerging, towelling my hair dry, casual, nothing on my mind save caffeine. She was dressed, a glass of Bush in her hand, asked,

"Join me?"

I tried not to sound like a total prick, going,

"Little early for me."

Sounded like a total prick. She knocked back the drink, said,

"You guys make neat booze."

Then,

"Wanna fuck?"

Pause.

"My apologies, like to make love?"

Then she was up, moving towards me, shoved the glass at me, said,

"Keep it in your shorts, fellah."

Banged the door on her way out.

I went back to bed, clean, if not easy.

The phone dragged me to consciousness, couldn't figure out where the hell was I? . . . But it was dark, grabbed the phone, muttered,

"Yeah?"

"Mr. Blake, you have a visitor, waiting in the lobby."

"Oh right, I'll be down, um, in ten minutes."

"As you wish, Mr. Blake."

Shit, I should have asked whom. Checked my watch, after ten, I'd been out fourteen hours, at least. Stumbled to the bathroom, got my head under the cold tap, woke me fast. Dried my hair, finger-combed it, get that raffish look. Put on a white shirt, jeans, the mocs, ready to roll. I shared the elevator with an elderly black man who gave me a warm smile, I said,

"How *you* doing?"

"I'm doing swell, young man, and thank *you* for asking."

New York, gotta love it.

I moved into the lobby and my brief joy evaporated. Juan. Dressed à la pimp. Bright . . . nay . . . blinding orange shirt and skintight white leather trousers, try that gear in Galway on a Saturday night, they'd chuck you in the Corrib. I thought,

"He's got to be fucking kidding."

Maybe heroin made you colour blind. He was wired, energy coursing through him, he asked,

"You ready to get down?"

Like we were a couple of frat boys, trying to be black. That's among the most pathetic things on the planet. I couldn't think of a sane answer, apart from "Aw, fuck," so said,

"Sure."

We went outside and there's a stretch limo, chauffeur holding the door, Juan said,

"For you, *hombre*, tonight you are the man."

When I didn't move, he said,

"Buddy of mine, runs a limo service, owes me big."

Tommy would have loved that crap. The bigger the nonsense, the more he dug it. A limo would light him up. I don't hate them but can't get over the ridiculous image they convey, plus, they call attention, which is the last item, like, ever, on my agenda. Juan bowed, said,

"After you, *amigo*."

I got in, saw a bucket of champagne on ice, full mini bar, and salsa on the speakers. Juan slid in beside me, asked,

"What's your poison, *muchacho*?"

I'd just got up, I wanted coffee, breakfast, solitude, said,

"I've been sleeping, need a caffeine fix."

He wasn't pleased, snapped at the intercom, rattled off some Spanish. The limo suddenly changed lanes and a few moments later, we pulled up. Through the window, I could see Starbucks; Juan asked,

"Watcha need?"

"Latte, shot of expresso."

Juan gave me a slow look, then fired off more orders. The driver was out and in flash time, was back, handed the container over. I placed it in a holder on the seat. Juan got out some cellophane packets, laid lines of white powder on the seat, rolled a bill, offered me. I shook my head and he snorted deep, three lines, let his head back, then made a sound midway between relief and agony. I began to work on the latte, I could see the coke hitting Juan, he mellowed, said,

"I want to say *muchas gracias, amigo.*"

"Yeah? Why's that."

"My woman, you took real good care of her."

I was glad of the cup, gave me something to work on, keep my head down, he continued:

"Some guys, they think maybe they can hit on her, I'm not around, they see a chance."

The coke hit another level and he used his index finger to rub his gums, said,

"They mess with my woman, I cut their nuts off."

Mister Mex macho. The expresso had jolted and the devil was in me to ask *how was it growing up in the Bronx*?"

Some reply was needed, so I tried,

"Juan, I don't think too many guys would want to mess with you."

Taking what Tommy called *the piss*, he took it as flattery, said,

"Sherry, she's *muy bonita, sí?*"

Testing me? I could play, fuck, had to, said,

"You've a good one there, she's . . . devoted."

His left leg was tapping out a rapid beat, not to the music, which mercilessly droned on, least not any external tape, this was pure nerves, fuelled on coke and adrenaline, he said,

"Sherry, she don't take to many *hombres*, they bore her, *comprende?* But you, you, *amigo*, she likes you, is good, no?"

I was in a minefield, tried,

"You guys been together long?"

Like I gave a goddamn.

Clicking his fingers, checking out his boots—looked like lizard skin, some creature's precious hide—he was off somewhere, then clicked back:

"Like a year, maybe, but is, you know, *siempre*, always, I got me some *señoritas* on the Lower East Side, no big thang (pronounced it thus) they is like . . . fuck babes, Sherry, she's my main event, she's my rock."

Some foundation.

I finished the coffee and he grabbed the cup, hit a button, and the window slid down, he chucked it out. Registering my surprise, he laughed.

"They can't take a joke, fuck 'em, right? . . . is important the limo is clean, is like life, keep the garbage outside."

I couldn't resist, said,

"Some philosophy."

He put up his hand, for the high five, I gave him my palm, feeling like a horse's ass, and he went,

"We're *simpatico*, you and me, bro, we gonna kick some ass."

Which was about as depressing news as I'd ever heard. There was a briefcase on the floor and he nudged it with his boot, said,

"Open it, my friend."

I gave him the look, said,

"Juan, I'm Irish, I don't open things without the bomb squad."

Took him a while to get it, then a display of teeth, the cokehead's smile, which has no connection to warmth. He tapped the case with the heel of his boot, so I picked it up, set it on my lap, lifted the top.

Guns.

Guys and guns.

Could be a musical.

Tommy was fascinated by them, always talking about *getting a piece.* I asked the obvious:

"Why?"

And got a look of total confusion, he said,

"You were in the army, don't you love weapons?"

I let out a deep breath, said,

"It's the very reason I have no use for them, put a dick-head and a gun together, you have a recipe for disaster."

The day I finally left the army, I'd figured on never having a gun in my possession again. Like so many other resolutions, it was only a matter of time. Tommy's love of weapons came from the movies; he said

"Man, if I was packing, I'd never be afraid."

I wanted to say that's when you most need to be afraid, asked,

"What are you afraid of?"

He gave the Irish answer:

"Bringlodi."

That's the Irish word for dreams. I was lost, asked,

"I'm not sure what you mean?"

He gave me the hangdog look, part anger, part sorrow, said,

"Steve, you're never sure what I mean, fuck, I'm not sure me own self, all I know is, my dreams scare the bejaysus out of me, and I'm afraid that one La Brea (fine day), the dreams will come true."

I'd heard him in the grip of his dreams, his body twisting and writhing, his teeth grinding, sweat rolling in torrents off him. There are few more awful sounds than the grinding of teeth, you know that deep trauma is the cause. Though his continued descent into the maelstrom of dope and booze pissed me off and alarmed me, I could understand why. Alas, comprehension didn't mean compassion or tolerance.

In a futile effort to get him off the fascination of guns, I'd said,

"Knowing you, you had a gun, you'd probably shoot yerself."

He'd gone real quiet and I thought maybe he hadn't heard me till he said,

"Not the worst scenario."

Tommy reached some basic part of me, some primitive need to protect. I'd promised his father I'd always watch out for him, and a pledge to a dying man in Ireland is the most binding contract you'll ever take. Seeing his face that time, contemplating suicide as an option, I made an oath to do whatever it took to keep him, if not safe, at least protected.

What gods there be, I think they especially love when you make such an undertaking. They send such grief down the pike that your very words will lodge and strangle in your throat.

As Juan displayed the hardware, the gleaming metal, I felt my throat muscles constrict. Making a supreme effort, I managed to actually look at the assembled tapestry of carnage.

I recognised a Glock 9 mill. The shiny black finish; holds seventeen rounds. One of those odd coincidences, I'd had one during the robbery. I lifted the second, heavy and made of silver aluminium alloy. A German SIG-Sauer, serious firepower. Juan said,

"Take your pick."

I said,

"Aren't we like, going to dinner?"

He didn't follow, gave a dubious,

"*Sí.*"

"So what, we're going to shoot them if the food sucks?"

He lunged at the case, grabbed the SIG, worked the slide, and feverishly jacked a round in the chamber, said,

"Fifteen rounds."

And I thought of one of my favourite Springsteen songs, "American Skin (41 Shots)."

I echoed,

"Fifteen rounds, what are you expecting?"

He ignored that, said,

"Pick one."

"No thanks."

He couldn't believe it, went,

"You're in America, you don't want to be armed?"

I shook my head, he hefted the SIG, trying to make sense of me, said,

"Not to have a gun . . . it's un-American."

Oh I wanted a gun, just not from him, asked,

"Where are we?"

All I could see was people wearing Gucci sneakers and rip-off Stella McCartney designs; he said,

"West Fifteenth."

"Didn't this used to be a shithole, meatpacking and male hookers?"

He shrugged.

"It changed, what are you going to do, now it's goddamn boutiques and freaking artists."

His cell phone chirped and he answered, launched into a spitting frenzy, banged it against the window, said,

"*Amigo*, I gotta take a rain check, one of my homies is in trouble."

"No big thing."

Truth is, I was relieved, I said,

"Drop me off here, I'll walk, get a feel again for the city."

He indicated the SIG and I shook my head.

The limo pulled over, I got out. Passersby didn't give me a second look, I could have been P. Diddy but no response; Juan said,

"Don't be a stranger, hear?"

Yeah, right.

I knew not taking the gun had been an insult. Too, I figured it had been some sort of test and I failed, like I gave a fuck. Ate in a diner, of all the reasons to live in America, they top the list, them and Johnny Cash.

"I feel the need. The need for speed."

— TOM CRUISE, "MAVERICK," *Top Gun*

STAPLETON WAS IN a safe house in Monaghan, he'd recently hijacked a shitpile of weapons. A bloody affair, he
lost three men and took two Brits down. Bad trade-off. He
was in serious stir with the Organisation, he was, to coin a
phase, a little too loose a cannon. And, he was hemorrhag-
ing money; men they could get, always another sucker willing to lie down for the cause but money, that was the life
pulse. One other man in the house with him, a Derry guy
named Dubh . . . the Irish for black . . . he was well-named,
his eyes were as dark as the mercy of the Paras. Like Stapleton, he'd started with the Stickies, the official IRA, then
when the split happened he'd joined the Provos but they
were bleating for peace, too, so he'd joined the newest most
ferocious offshoot, the Patriots. He was fascinated by hardware and spent hours cleaning the weapons, studying the
manuals, loading and unloading. He actually polished the
ammunition, with loving care. Stapleton had joked,

"You need to get out more, *cara* (mate)."

And got a look he'd have been proud to display himself. Dubh was his kind of guy but a rarity now, literally a dying breed. He was drinking a large Jameson, bottle of stout as chaser, said, giving the black liquid the evil eye,

"Not the same out of a bottle, is it?"

Stapleton was tempted to say,

"You're having no problems with the Jameson."

Cooped up with a guy for who knew how long, you didn't want to sour the air, so he nodded. He had a mug of tea himself, heavily sweetened, he surely liked his tea, or cha, as his mother used to call it. Dubh's tongue was loosened by the booze and he was as close to loquacious as he'd ever be, asked,

"You ever watch pictures?"

He meant movies, but being old Ireland he hadn't yet adopted *movies* or any of the other Americanisms. All the freedom fighters were video literate, not from choice but from enforced confinement, in Long Kesh or safe houses. 'Nam movies were hugely popular, and of course, *Michael Collins, In the Name of the Father, Harry's Game.* Stapleton didn't watch, preferred to listen to music but only as background. He was constantly on the alert for the Brit patrols, how the hell were you going to hear a helicopter if you were watching Robert Duvall doing his own chopper riff. Dubh, more to himself, continued:

"Me, I like Jim Cameron, *The Terminator, Aliens*, all that fucking hardware and you know, it looks used. Cameron, I tell you, he knows his stuff, he was on the verge of inventing a pulse gun by joining a Thompson submachine gun with a Franchi SPAS-twelve pump-action shotgun."

Stapleton glanced at him, the guy's eyes shining, fired on visions of carnage, he was near orgasmic,

"It was based on the Spandau MG 42 with thermal imagery sights."

Stapleton was almost moved, here was a young man, his whole life shaped by violence, the only thing to excite him being the talk and dreams of weapons, the deadlier the better. Elsewhere in the country, young men were talking about Gaelic football, hurling, women, dances, cars, and Saturday nights at the pub. Dubh would only ever drink in shebeens, the illegal establishments run by the Boyos and where the smell of cordite was as familiar as the kegs of Smithwick's brought in from Dundalk.

A few weeks later, Dubh would be shot in the head by the most basic rifle available, nothing fancy, no laser sight or even thermal capability, it killed him instantly, Stapleton felt that was irony of the most Protestant style, i.e., vicious.

Like James Cameron desperately needing *Titanic* to come in mega, Stapleton needed a big hit. He was running out of time, cash, and credibility. His master plan was to hit south of the border and involve Southerners, patsies who'd take the fall, involve the Republic and, best of all, grab the fucking euros to finance the Northern campaign.

His plan was fairly simple: get hold of some dumb guy from the Republic, do a couple of gigs in the North, get him a taste for it, then go south, hit big there, kill the idiot and get the hell out, leave Southern fingerprints all over it. How hard could it be? Belfast was crawling with starry-eyed youngsters who'd come over the border, wanting the romance of the cause, wanted to carry weapons and attain that sheen of patriotism they'd acquired more from Hollywood movies than Irish history.

He fully intended to make them history.

He remembered his father, before the Brits took him out, a tall man, always speaking in Irish, with a Fainne in his lapel. It was the gold badge awarded to Irish speakers who spoke fluently. When they'd put the riddled body in the casket, Stapleton had leaned over, took the pin from his dad's only suit. He used to wear it but it was a dead give away for the Brits, so he carried it in his wallet, alongside the old currency of the South, the punts, the green notes with herself on them.

The volunteers nowadays, they wore frigging earrings, like nancy boys. Not on his watch they didn't. A young fellow from Fermanagh had a stud in his left ear, Stapleton ripped it out, said,

"You're a man, an Irish man, have some fucking dignity."

And . . . they watched soccer, Jaysus . . . and even betimes . . . rugby. So okay, Manchester United had a huge Irish history but the beautiful game was killing the Gaelic. Stapleton had been a ferocious hurler. His own honed stick, from the ash, complete with the steel bands on the end, was among his proudest possessions. He'd broken it across the back of an informer. The dreaded snitch, now elevated to supergrass . . . selling out their comrades for money and to save their own wretched skins. He heard there was some American band called Supergrass . . . he wouldn't be listening for them anytime soon. The supergrass, a term coined by the English press, a man who'd sell his own mother, and indeed, their like had been the cause of a lot of good men going down. Then, they became discredited and had to be whisked away to save the blushes of the Brits.

When Stapleton had still been a regular part of the campaign and they were being decimated by the traitors, his unit caught one of them.

Young guy, twenty years of age, looked like the punk he was. After he'd been through the water, cigarettes, testicles routines, they gave him to Stapleton. He took him to a shack on the outskirts of the city, the kid, whinging, hurting, terror in his eyes. Stapleton had to contain the rage of his men who wanted the old-style punishment, tar and feathers.

Like it was yesterday, Stapleton could summon the scene effortlessly. Put a blanket round the lad, who was shivering, asked,

"Want a cup of tea, drop of the creature in it?"

The wretch, his teeth bloody stumps, nodded, desperate for any bit of kindness. Stapleton clicked his fingers and one of his unit went to fetch it, pissed in the cup after he added the Jameson. Stapleton had to hold the cup to the fellow's lips, his tremors were so bad. He hunkered down, asked,

"Know where that blanket comes from?"

The kid, confusion in his eyes, looked at the grey material, pulled it round him tighter, as if it would protect him, echoed,

"Blanket?"

The guys from the unit had gathered round, an opportunity to see the legendary Stapleton at work, they weren't much impressed, yet. Stapleton said,

"What you've got there is a piece of living history, a

blanket from Long Kesh, part of the dirty protest, you smell it, you can still get the shite they used to daub the walls."

The kid tried to shrug it off; Stapleton was up, walked away, then returned with his old hurly, swinging it, hearing the roars of the crowd as a Northern county took the All Ireland title from the south, he said,

"And this, this is your legacy, you like sport?"

Despite the warmth of his words, the friendliness, a chill had entered the enclosed space, the kid stammered,

"Liver . . . Liverpool . . . Gerard . . ."

Never got to finish as Stapleton swung light and loose, the stick taking the kid full in the mouth, Stapleton, continuing in his easy tone,

"Fucking Brit game . . ."

Whack.

The kid's jaw.

"Now, hurling, we've been playing it for centuries . . ."

The kid's body doubled as the hurly shattered his kneecaps. Five minutes of intensive beating, the swish of the stick, Stapleton's mini history of the growth of Irish sport, and all the while, the measured quiet words, as the young body was battered to mush.

When one of the guys in the unit finally took the hurly from Stapleton's bloody hands, the shaft had actually ruptured and grey matter clung to the end. They buried the kid in a shallow grave, Stapleton flung the stick in, too, muttered,

"May you roast in hell, you treacherous cunt."

That's who Stapleton was.

"It Ain't Cool to Be Crazy About You"

— GEORGE STRAIT

NEXT DAY, I hailed a cab, went to Ground Zero. Nothing had prepared me, not the newspapers, the TV images, seeing the sheer emptiness devastated me. I tried to read the notices honouring the dead but had to turn away. The enormity of the loss was too much to grasp and I walked, as fast as I could.

I don't know how long I strode but gradually my mind refocused and I saw Rosie O'Grady's, went in, and the barman said,

"How are you doing, sir?"

Sir!

I said I was good and could I have a large Seagram's, water back. He placed it before me and I took a hefty belt, waited for it to mellow me out.

It did.

Easing out a suppressed breath, I shook my head to clear

the images. Tommy, going, the first time he saw the Towers,
   "Fucking hell."

Tommy wasn't easily impressed, worked at taking everything as no big deal, kept the world low key. His home life had been chaotic and his anger he'd converted into feigned indifference. We'd grown up on the same street and been friends from the off, during my college years, I'd often tried to pair him with various women. He'd say *sure* and then behave so badly they never lasted. Over pints, late, after my final exams, he'd said,
   "You know, Steve, I never had a good idea in my life."

I was the worse for wear, that hour when maudlin is dangerously close, said,
   "Hey buddy, you came to Dublin, how bad was that?"

Sometimes, the more he drank, the more sober he appeared, he thought about what I said, then,
   "Naw, I'd no place to go, you're the only direction I ever had."

Like I said, maudlin.

I'd clapped his arm, tried the Irish solution, asked,
   "You want some Jameson?"

Shook his head, then,
   "I don't get it."

"Get what?"

"Life."

I laughed out loud, went,
   "Shit, buddy, no one gets it, what do you think these pubs are for?"

He wasn't buying, said,
   "You do, Steve, you're a player, always in control. And if you cut loose, I think it's because you get bored, you like to

shake it up but you only visit the edge, you don't live there, and see . . ."

He took a deep breath, this was more analysis than Tommy ever did, then,

"See, after you do some mad bollix of a thing, you scuttle back to safety. You can do that, I know as I've seen you do it so often."

His voice was loud, a hint of hysteria, it was late, way past closing time and we were part of that cherished tradition *after hours*. The barman gave us a look of warning, not because a raised voice bothered him but lest we draw the Guards. Tommy continued:

"What I want to know is, how do you do that shit?"

I leant over, advised,

"Keep it down, buddy."

He sat back, a triumphant smile on his face, said,

"There you go, case proved."

I don't know what time we got out of there, I'd trotted a line of clichés, hackneyed phrases, and he'd stopped in the middle of Grafton Street, said,

"It's okay, Steve, you can ease up, life's a joke, just sometimes, I'm not in the mood for laughing."

We never went as deep again. On some very basic level, I hadn't reassured him, who could? That we might have connected on some instinctive stage hadn't happened. Odd times, I'd try to get us back there, back to the raw emotion of being lost, but the book was closed. As if we'd taken a look at his very soul and found it bare. So he distanced it, made a decision to party on, even if he was an unwanted guest.

A few times, I caught an expression in his eyes, not lost

but frustrated. He'd adopted the Irish version of fatalism—
fecklessness. When you just don't give a toss. We even had
a prayer for it, albeit a Galway one, a softer sound than
fuckit, we said . . . feckit.

Kept it almost light but the intention was clear. The hell
with it all and let the devil take the consequences. On a
toilet wall, I saw it expressed best: *The lord gave me no
class, let the devil give me style.* After we returned from
America, Tommy said,

"Biggest mistake we ever made."

"What's that, then?"

As if I didn't know.

He sighed, raising his hands in mock defeat, said,

"Coming back."

My mother was dying, I'd little choice. Had tried to per-
suade him to remain in America, to no avail.

I'd said,

"Soon as we get our shit together, we're like outta here,
deal?"

He looked me straight, said,

"I'm never going to get back."

He was right.

My mother was an alcoholic. Ten years of age, I'd be
knocking down the door of the local pub, an empty baby of
Paddy Power in my hand. The publican, he'd open the
door, sigh at the sight of me, we'd done this dance a lot,
take the bottle, and go,

"On the slate, right?"

Meaning, no money.

My face, scarlet with shame, my stomach, sick with

anxiety, I'd want to pee. Then, he'd return, hand over the bottle, full to the brim, and slam the door. There'd be other callers, all morning long, but none as early as me.

The slate was the salvation or damnation of our neighbourhood, depending on which side of the financial fence you fell. Another word for it was *tick*, an early form of credit card and just as mercenary. Fixed penalties to the grave and beyond; every so often, my father would drop into the pub, lay a wedge on the counter, and the publican took it without comment. Exact figures were never discussed, the only certainty was nobody gained from the deal, least not in any fashion that entailed dignity.

My father liked a pint, come Friday night, he'd go out, have three, play rings, come home. At a wedding, he might have a glass of Redbreast. It was said of my mother, she had "nerves."

And she fucking needed them. Took all her ability to function and present some semblance of normality. Twice, she lost it, big-time and they carted her off to Ballinasloe, no rehab then.

Ward 8, the asylum snake pit. They tied you a chair and let the alcohol scream and pour from you. Used a hose to wash you down. I know about Ward 8, as my mother, half in the bag, gave me a full and horrific account. At school, I'd be taunted,

"Your oul wan's in the madhouse . . . again."

Tommy would launch himself on the accuser and I'd stand, frozen by the word "again." Till Tommy incited me to use my fists, my legs, hit back.

The taunts stopped but the terror only receded, lying in wait to reappear.

My mother didn't drink for the last two years of her life. Stayed sober with a grim determination and a near hysterical control, that's where I learned that icy talent. No one knows where she got the pills, as visits to a doctor were rare and, worse, expensive. But she was an alcoholic, cunning was second nature. I was in New York, making serious money on the site, and she'd collected, amassed over fifty sleepers.

Didn't kill her right off, she went into a semi-coma, took a week to die. What they call "a hard death."

Her face a rictus of agony and her body motionless. I returned to witness most of this. If my father hadn't been mounting a twenty-four-hour vigil, I'd have put a pillow on her face. He held her limp hand and said decades of the rosary, like that made a difference to either of them

She gave a tiny whisper of breath on a Thursday morning and gave it up. I often hear that slight breath, like a sigh. I didn't cry and I'm not crying now.

I'm glad she's dead.

Sitting now in a New York bar, a large drink in my hand, I remembered how often she'd implored me,

"Promise me you won't drink, Stephen."

Yeah, right.

There's a line in *The Colossus Of New York: A City in 13 Parts*, by Colson Whitehead, "Maybe we become New Yorkers the day we realize that New York will go on without us." I asked myself . . . *if maybe Tommy is finally buried the day I realize life goes on without him*? As they'd say back home, perish the thought.

The barman asked,

"Hit you again?"

And I nodded. Memory has a hold like that on you, you better have hold of something equally lethal, a gun or a bottle. The barman gave me a friendly smile, asked,

"On vacation?"

"No."

Shut him down. I wanted a new friend, I wasn't going to get one in a bar. I was running a tab and he looked like he wanted to say something but turned, went off to do bar stuff.

The evening Tommy said,

"I'm going to be gone for a bit."

I made light of it, tried,

"Bro, you've been gone for years."

Didn't fly.

And he didn't smile. We were in a new apartment I'd rented, along by the canal. On the top floor, you looked out, you could see the ducks. He said,

"I'm serious."

Like a horse's ass, I wouldn't go with, persisted,

"Tommy, serious isn't what you do, that's my gig, re-member?"

I was beginning to irritate him and myself, so added,

"You mean it?"

"Yeah, I'm in a bit of bother, it's best if I go out of town, let the heat ebb."

Ebb.

I wanted to say I'd go with him, but I'd just met Siobhan, my father was alone and hurting and . . . and . . . I didn't want to go, said,

"Is it money, what?"

He waved his hand, dismissive, went,

"It's shit is what it is, I need to be on my own, see how I do."

He'd do terrible; even with me riding shotgun, he didn't do so well. Veered from flush to broke and all stops in between. His drug intake was upped alarmingly, from Valium (daily basis) through speed to evenings on coke. It showed. His face was gaunt, he'd lost a ton of weight, and his nerves, his nerves were fucked.

I'd seen him low many times, it was what Tommy did, not so much hit bottom as bounce off it, then somehow gouge back to a level of . . . if not normality, then maintenance. But now, his whole spirit seemed crushed, I had to jack up his tyres, tried the old bullshit, near sang,

"Hey, bro, we're buddies right? . . . semper fi and all that marine gung ho. We're the O.K. Corral, backs against the fence, still firing."

He shook his head, asked,

"You remember a song, old song . . . had a line . . . *getting mighty tired of southern comfort . . .?*"

Took me a moment, well longer, then, I finished the line:

"*Go north.*"

He smiled sadly, then,

"You always know, don't you Steve, always?"

The penny dropped, he was going over the border. For our generation, like the ones who went before, going north meant only one thing.

Deep shit.

TOMMY WAS GONE for nine months. I got intermittent calls that told me little, save he was wired, I asked if I could come see him but no way. Whenever I tried to probe, he'd cut the connection. A guy I knew had set up a music shop, a small operation but he needed assistance. I wasn't doing a whole lot, so said I'd help out. Began with two days a week then got interested and ended up doing six, getting a real buzz. I was seeing Siobhan regularly and we were comfortable, easy round each other. My life settled into a routine that was the signal for me to glance towards the abyss.

Tommy returned, bringing if not hell with him, then certainly its embodiment.

Stapleton.

I was at home, seven in the evening, watching *The Simpsons*, Siobhan asked,

"Why do guys love Homer?"

You need to ask?

The phone went, I picked up, heard,

"I'm back."

"Tommy! That's great, come round, we'll—"

"I'm not alone."

I immediately jumped to a conclusion, the wrong one, went,

"Great, bring her round."

A pause, and I had to go,

"Tommy, you still there?"

"It's not a woman, it's a . . . a guy, a fellah I've been working with."

His tone was flat and I knew there was something amiss, said,

"Well, okay, we can do men, Siobhan and I will come meet you guys, where you at?"

"Garavan's."

One of the great old unchanged pubs.

"Right, say half an hour."

"Steve . . ."

"Yeah?"

"Come alone."

Click.

I relayed the conversation to Siobhan and she said,

"That's odd."

Which turned out to be some understatement. I put on a leather jacket I'd bought in New York, in the East Village. It looked beat up, shit it *was* beat up, leather fraying on the collar. Seemed appropriate. I kissed Siobhan, like I meant it, said,

"I won't be late."

She fixed the collar, licked her hand, patted down my hair, said,

"I've a bad feeling about this."

"It'll be fine."

I was wrong.

They were in the snug. Garavan's is one of the very few establishments that hasn't moved on, time has stood still, thank Christ. Among its many blessings no muzak is one of the top. Tommy looked shagged, he'd grown his hair, it looked lank and, yeah, dirty. His weight had gone way down and his cheekbones bulged against the skin. He was wearing a combat jacket, the pockets overflowing. Pints of Guinness, shorts, lined the table. You'd have thought *party* save for the atmosphere. Heavy and lethal.

The man beside Tommy was also in a combat jacket. Older, in his fifties, with a shaved head. The light bounced off it, sending dark illumination. Sallow skin with deep ridges down his cheeks. Lots of lines round the eyes but you'd never call them laughter lines. A nose that'd been broken more than once, and oddly, a full sensual mouth. A livid scar across his forehead.

He had brown eyes with the oddest aspect, as if he were sleepy, one beat from closing down. They carried no message at all and that was worrying. Tommy said,

"Steve."

I waited, expecting him to stand, get a hug. Wasn't happening. He added without looking at him,

"This is Stapleton."

I put out my hand and it hung there, no one rushed to hold it, I let it fall to my side, Tommy said,

"We got you a pint."

Then the worst, he giggled. Not a suppressed laughter or god forbid, even what writers call a chuckle, no, a fucking giggle. Like some ten-year-old schoolgirl and said,

"Fuck, we got you lots of pints."

I said,

"Hey, maybe the timing's off, I'll hook up with you to-morrow."

Stapleton said,

"Don't be a bollocks, sit down."

An order.

I looked at him, he seemed to be enjoying a private joke, so I asked,

"Was I talking to you?"

Tommy let out a deep breath, went,

"Whoops, it's not going well."

Stapleton stared at me, no discernible change in his eyes, said,

"You're the guy took the king's shilling."

There it was.

Hundreds of years of history in one line. The insult used to describe a turncoat, an Irishman who enlisted in the British army. All the very worst of our past was contained there, informers, traitors, betrayal.

The usual translation . . . scum of the earth. I looked at Tommy, asking

"You told him that?"

And what else? Tommy lowered his eyes, grabbed a short, knocked it back. I turned back to Stapleton, said,

"And that's your concern, how?"

He laughed, shoved a stool with his boot, said,

"Lighten up, partner, just be grateful we're not in Belfast."

Then he supped noisily at his pint, looked up, asked,

"Blake, didn't those turncoats pretend to be Protestant to save their property?"

The Catholic gentry had converted to the Protestant faith in an effort to retain their lands. It was widely believed that they continued to practice as Catholics.

The most famous story involved Sir Thomas Blake. On his deathbed, he asked for a Catholic priest and his Protestant relatives refused. When the funeral reached the graveyard, the Catholic tenants barred the Protestants from entry. Widespread violence was the inevitable result.

I was reared Catholic but of course, lurking in my history was the Blake inheritance. Going to Trinity, joining the British army seemed to prove the old adage *what's bred in the blood, breaks out in the bone.*

I had no reply to that, leastways none that came without violence, so I said to Tommy,

"You ever sober up, give me a call."

And walked out.

Could hear Stapleton's derisory laughter behind.

I had no idea what to do about Tommy; I laid it out for Siobhan and she said,

"Do nothing."

That's what I did. The music shop was staring to develop. We'd brisk trade in secondhand stock. Mike, the guy I worked for, did the boring stuff, kept the books, did invoices, and I got to stock the cool guys, Cash, Strummer, Tom Russell. Was drooling over an early Tom Waits album when I heard,

"Music pays?"

Turned to face Tommy, he'd cleaned up, his clothes, anyway. Wearing a new crisp white shirt and a full-length suede jacket. He'd made the effort. Hard to clean up the eyes, so he was wearing tinted glasses. I said,

"What, you're modelling for Gap?"

A light sheen of perspiration on his brow, the morning coke blues. He asked,

"Want to get a drink?"

Couldn't help it, I looked at my watch and he asked,

"How tight is your timetable?"

An edge to it and I said,

"Eleven o' clock, bit early for it."

He looked over his shoulder, said,

"I checked with your boss, he can spare you, for like, twenty minutes, I'll time you, how would that be?"

We'd never fenced like this before, had been through highs, lows, like any close relationship, but never hit this level of sniping, I said,

"He's not my boss."

Tommy shrugged.

"Whatever, you coming or not?"

Truth is, I didn't want to go. The months he'd been away, I got used to the relative calm. Sure, my nature wanted to cut loose but not as fiercely as before. I realised how much work Tommy was. The constant veering, reeling from crisis to half-baked resolution and the mountains of dope, the killer hangovers. I'd begun to admit, what I never would have acknowledged, Tommy was a pain in the ass. I grabbed my jacket and we were out of there. Tommy gave a nod to the Galway Arms and, reading my face, said,

"They do coffee . . . and hey, maybe herbal tea."

They'd just opened and we caught a corner table, large window to our left. A blast of rare sunshine illuminated us, giving an appearance of cheerfulness. I asked,

"Get you?"

"Coffee . . . black."

I knew the owner and he said,

"Your shop is doing mighty."

Irish hyberbole at its finest but what the hell, it wasn't noon yet, I could hack it, said,

"Not too bad alright."

This covers everything from franchising to bankruptcy. He poured the coffee, asked,

"You have any of the Clancy Brothers?"

I had no idea, said,

"Sure, I'll put them aside for you."

I reached for my wallet and he waved it away with,

"Ary, a drop of coffee, won't break the bank."

The odd moments, you meet a human being, you feel life might be liveable. Back at the table, Tommy was trying to light a cig, I emphasise trying. He'd got the thing in his mouth, had a lighter but the next link in the chain seemed to have eluded him, I snapped,

"You take off the shades, you might see what you're doing."

Sounded even harsher than I meant. I'd leaned on *shades*, getting a hefty helping of scorn on there, he said,

"Can't."

"What, they're glued to your face?"

No disguising my anger now, out there like a palpable force. You watch your closest friend go down the toilet, you better be agitated. As if to show me, he raised the hand with the lighter and it shook like the stage in Riverdance. I grabbed the lighter, feeling his hand slick with sweat, said,

"Gimme the bloody thing."

Fired him up. He took a massive hit of nicotine and I was thinking of Ginsberg's "Howl" . . ."*I saw the best minds of my generation destroyed by madness.*"

Wanted to howl myself, Tommy said,

"I'm sorry, bro."

"Hey, no big thing."

But it was.

He stood and I thought he was going to bolt, God forgive me, I'd have been relieved and I certainly wouldn't have followed, he said,

"Gotta pee."

He was gone, like ten minutes. My cup was empty, his coffee had died, got that shiny top like a rancid pool. I was on the verge of going for him when he returned. First thing I noticed, the shades were off and his eyes were . . . not alive but electrified. And he was Mr. Affability, slid into his seat, said,

"That's better, you know me Steve, mornings are not my strong point, takes me a time to catch up with you guys."

This said in a rush, the words nearly colliding, tumbling out of his mouth like pistons. Then I saw the traces of white powder on his left nostril. What to do, let it slide, act like this was hunky dory. Did I? Did I fuck. Reached over, used my thumb to wipe it, said,

"Missed a bit, want to snort it?"

He lifted his cup, drank the cold brew, no shake visible, said,

"You didn't used to be so tight assed."

"You didn't used to be so seriously fucked."

Silence then as the pieces of our friendship danced and dipped, trying to move us from a veritable split. I asked,

"What's with this Stapleton?"

Tommy shifted his position to escape the sunlight, said,

"He doesn't like you."

"Gee, that's worrying."

"I'm serious, Steve, he really doesn't like you."

"Hey, I heard you, alright?"

I looked at my watch, becoming addicted to the gesture, Tommy went,

"I owe him big."

"Pay him off, just get rid of him."

Shaking his head,

"It's not simply money." He took a deep breath, then,

"We're going to take down a bank."

"What, are you nuts, in Galway? They have the army doing security and hey, hello, those guys are seriously armed."

As if he didn't hear, he said,

"We always have a third guy but he's . . . am . . . indisposed."

I let it sink in, waited for more and when it wasn't coming, said,

"Oh no, you've got to be kidding, you think I'd get involved?"

His head was down and in a low voice, he said,

"I said you'd help."

"You stupid bastard. Go tell them you were mistaken."

Now he leaned across the table, grabbed my arm, pleaded,

"Steve, you refuse and I'm dead."

Another twenty minutes we went at it, round and round and always back to the same conclusion. Finally I said,

"Okay. But this better be nailed down solid, you hear?"

He nodded, then,

"It's next Wednesday, that's when they move a motherlode."

"Fuck."

"Mammas, Don't Let Your Babies Grow Up To Be Cowboys."

— WILLIE NELSON

I **SNAPPED OUT** of my reverie. Replaying Tommy's death—I couldn't go there yet, not so soon after visiting Ground Zero. I visualised Siobhan and the way she might look at you, those eyes always on the alert for betrayal. She wasn't the proverbial deer caught in headlights—she'd been bodily lifted and set down in rush hour traffic.

Her great and maybe only friend was a girl she'd trained in the bank with, Kaitlin, they were same age but radically different in every other way. Kaitlin was party animal and complete extrovert. Siobhan was always the quiet one, intense, preoccupied. Kaitlin had not been, as they say, blessed in the looks department. As close to ugly as it gets and a serious weight problem. If it bothered her, and it must have, she hid it well. I had rarely met a person of such genuine good nature. When you get two girls as tight they were and then one finds a partner, a certain distance ensues.

Not with them.

Siobhan always made certain she saw Kaitlin twice a week. They'd have what has become known as the girls' night out and they'd hit a pub, do some concentrated drinking. Siobhan didn't drink much around me and I'd asked,

"What's with that, you get plastered with Kaitlin, then play Miss Mormon with me?"

She'd stared at me, not in an angry way but that focused expression of weighing what I'd asked. You never got a fast reply from her but it was always the truth, whether you liked it or not; she'd said,

"With you, I want to savour every minute, drink would blur that, Kaitlin is an open book to me, drunk or sober, I know her and like her, I need to let the devils out every so often."

I made the mistake of sharing this with Tommy, who went,

"Horseshite."

What did I expect?

Kaitlin got the opportunity to transfer to New York and took it. She wasn't the type of girl to agonise over decisions, she acted fast. We threw a party for her departure and like the tradition of our ancestors, piled up with booze. Siobhan had bought her a gold Claddagh brooch, cost a week's wages, I bought her a Saint Bridget's Cross.

They're supposed to keep your home safe; Mike, who owned the music store, told me he'd had one and when his home was robbed, the only thing they took was the cross. I didn't share this with Kaitlin.

A lot of people came and it was one lively affair. The

Saw Doctors were on the turntable, and Kaitlin, her face flushed, grabbed my hand, said,

"Dance with me."

I did. . . . badly.

The Saw Doctors were from Tuam, the song playing was that mad "Joyce Country Ceili Band." Kaitlin was like Siobhan, a fine dancer, and went into an impromptu jig followed by a reel. That finished and was followed by "Share the Darkness." I hoped it wasn't an omen. Sweat pouring down her face, Kaitlin pulled me close, said,

"Yer wan will kill me."

Meaning Siobhan. I made some inane comment, trying not to step on her toes. Kaitlin said,

"She's mad about you."

How to reply to this, getting gratitude and disbelief into the reply. You go the other way, act like it's no surprise, and an Irish woman will cut you off at the knees, literally. They don't do smugness, not well, anyway. I said,

"I'm lucky to have found her."

I meant it.

Kaitlin took my hand, said,

"Let's get a jar."

She had a Harvey Wallbanger and I was drinking Jameson, neat. We clinked glasses, said,

"Slainte."

The place was packed, I could see Siobhan talking to some people and Kaitlin said,

"You always check to see where she is and believe me, she does the same, that's fecking mighty, wish I'd a fellah who cared where I was."

I did what you do, muttered about how anyone would be

lucky to have her and of course, she'd definitely find someone, the banalities of social nicety, I'm not good at it and
find it rough going but I liked her enough to at least take a
shot at it. She laughed, said,

"Jaysus, you're a terrible liar but thanks for the thought,
in New York I'm going to bag me a fireman or a cop, they
love Irish girls, don't they?"

I agreed they did and she was quiet for a second then,

"And they're used to people with weight."

Tommy was veering in our direction and Kaitlin went,

"Oh oh, trouble, what do you see in that ejit?"

I told the truth, said,

"He's my friend."

She waved that off, said,

"He's baggage and you'd need to watch yerself, that fellah, he'll bring the gates of hell wherever he goes."

She nailed that right.

She grabbed my hand, said,

"Siobhan is very fragile, all that strength she displays, it
comes at a cost, she'd take a bullet for you, you need to
mind her, won't you do that, won't you mind her?"

I swore I would and just as Tommy fell on us, she stood,
said,

"My public awaits."

Tommy was four sheets to the wind, per usual, and
glared at Kaitlin, his eyes were out of focus, he had a large
whiskey in his fist, larger amounts in his system, he
slurred,

"She hates me."

I don't know which is worse, the maudlin drunk with
the huge dollop of self-pity or the aggressive one. Least the

aggressive one, you can give him a slap in the mouth, you wallop the whiner, you prove his point, I snapped,

"Fuck's sake, everything isn't about you."

He grabbed my arm, said,

"You hate me, too."

Right then, he was correct, I sighed, went,

"She doesn't even know you, so give it a rest."

Set him off properly:

"Nobody knows me."

But god is good, Tommy let his head back, and passed out. The evening was a late one and we parted from Kaitlin with the usual pledges of staying in touch, the desperate hugs, the reluctance to finally say good-bye. That night in bed, I hugged Siobhan close, said,

"I'm going to mind you."

She laughed, said,

"Just because you promised Kaitlin."

Women . . . Jesus.

Shook myself, and was back at the bar in New York, thinking, "Christ, gimme a break."

A shot of bourbon in my hand, did I really want to be hurting?

No.

The booze had lit a fire in my belly, giving me that artificial calm, and I knew how easy I could hammer down a few more. How difficult is it? Lock and load. All the arguments about alcoholism and the question, is it hereditary? The serious drinkers I've met—and being Irish, I've met a lot, came from parents who put it away big-time. Till it put them away. I was pretty sure I carried the gene. Thus my huge effort always for control. So I pushed my glass away, the bar guy asked,

"You done?"

I nodded and paid the tab, leaving a hefty tip. He acknowledged it but didn't like me a whole lot better. I was out of there and figured I'd call it a night. At the hotel, I collected the key, headed for the elevator. The bellboy was passing and avoided my eyes. What was that about? Was I supposed to slip him a ten every time we met? Fuck that. Got to my room, went in, and Sherry was in bed, sitting up, went,

"Nearly started without you."

Jesus, what if Juan had been with me? I kept my voice neutral.

"How'd you get in?"

"The bellboy."

"What, you palm him twenty bucks?"

She gave me a look of pure scorn, went,

"I don't give men bribes, least not in cash."

"So, you gave him some story, that it?"

She tapped the space beside her, said,

"Come on lover, I'm dying here."

When I didn't move, she said,

"I promised him a blow job, he near shot his wad right there."

I wish I could say I threw her out. But she'd gotten under my skin. I knew little about love but plenty about heat and she was it. Later, dressing, she asked,

"You're like outta here, am I right?"

"What?"

"You're blowing New York, I can tell."

I was tempted to say she was the expert on blowing but let it slide, too easy, said,

"No, I like it here."

She was dressed now, her hand on the door, said,

"We call it Two-son."

"What?"

"Where you're headed, know why, no building over two stories, it's a cowboy town, think you can handle that?"

Yet again I cursed the brochures on Tucson I'd left lying around. To distract her, I offered,

"Let me spring for cab fare."

Implying a warmth I didn't feel. She produced a hundred dollar bill, said,

"You already did."

Not sure what this meant but fairly certain it meant only one thing, and not wanting confirmation, I stared at her. She said,

"I went through your wallet, who's the babe?"

A photo of Siobhan, from a day on the beach at Spiddal, another lifetime, Sherry had the door opened, parted with,

"You go to Tucson cowboy, I'll follow you."

And was gone.

So was the photo of Siobhan.

Five hundred bucks, too. The term "bunny boiler" rose alarmingly in my mind, remembering Glen Close's scorned, "don't-fuck-with-her" character in *Fatal Attraction*. I went to the bathroom. In the toilet bowl were fragments of the photo. No two ways about it, I'd bought myself a shitpile of trouble.

In the corridor, late afternoon, I met the bellboy, stopped, said,

"You let anyone in my room again, I'll throw you out the window."

He looked round, as if for help, said,

"She said she was like, you know, your wife."

He'd a whine in his voice, the eternal "blame it on the other guy scenario," and I asked,

"We clear?"

He nodded. I got in the elevator, thought,

"Nice work, Steve, intimidating the help."

New York was slipping away from me. The control I prized was frayed in all directions. As I got to the street, a limo pulled up, the driver leaned out, said,

"Yo, mister, Juan says I'm to drive you, wherever you wish."

"Fuck off."

Time to phone Siobhan. We'd agreed I'd wait a few days, let me get settled. Yeah, like I was already settled now. Bought a prepaid card and now, all I had to do was find a phone that worked. Third attempt, got one. Punched in the digits, waited, then heard the Irish lilt,

"Yes?"

Lit me up. I near gagged at how much I loved her. Guilt over Sherry was nagging away. I said,

"Hi, hon."

"Stephen, are you okay?"

Lie, lie a lot, Tommy's theme. I said,

"I'm fine but I miss you."

Which I did and I'd spent my whole life guarding against such a vulnerability. You were vulnerable, they ate you up, spat you out. She sounded hesitant, something in her voice, and I asked,

"Hon, anything wrong?"

"No, it's probably, I'm just being silly but,"

I locked on the money, thinking *fuck*, thinking *it's got to go through*, asked,

"The transfers?"

"No, no, that's fine, you know how good I am at my job."

She was a financial whiz kid. When I'd told her the amount I needed "laundered," she'd frowned and I figured she couldn't do it till she laughed, said,

"This is so exciting."

Now she paused, then,

"I saw Stapleton."

I tried,

"Maybe you were mistaken."

She considered and I could see her, the small frown she got when something was wrong, something her fiscal talent couldn't fix, then,

"Yeah, maybe."

Stapleton wasn't really the kind of guy who looked like anyone else. He didn't stand out in a crowd, he was too clever for that. You saw him, it was for one reason, he wanted it, I asked,

"We could move up the timetable, get you over sooner."

I knew she wouldn't go for that. She said,

"And screw up the transfer, I've worked hard on this, it's going exactly as I planned. I leave it now, it could blow up. I need to be here, ensure I'm the one overseeing the deal."

She was right, someone else might look a little too closely at the amount of money and worse, where the hell it came from. The whole delicate process rested on Siobhan being in charge. I said,

"You see him again . . ."

"I'm not sure it was him."

"You haul ass."

She laughed and I asked what was funny. She said,

"You're doing it, talking American."

"Yeah, it's getting there."

She laughed again, coquettish now, asked,

"Here's one I learned, getting your ashes hauled, you miss that?"

"Do I ever."

The credit was running low and I said,

"Gra go mor." (huge love)

"Leat fein." (you too)

Click.

Holding the dead phone, I had a moment of forlornness. Washed over me like the Galway rain when you're least prepared. A guy waiting, went,

"You going to hog that all day, buddy?"

Automatically I said,

"Sorry."

And he grabbed the phone, said,

"Yeah, everybody's goddamn sorry."

I moved away lest the temptation to make him eat it proved too attractive, stopped at a diner, grabbed a booth, and the waitress goes,

"How are you today, young man?"

A winner, right?

I granted I was good, ordered hash browns, eggs over easy, bagel, the ubiquitous coffee.

While I waited, a story came into my head, one Tommy had told me over hot toddies one evening. We'd gone to Furbo to hear a band, renowned for their mix of rock and traditional. Into the heart of Connemara, a turf fire in the lounge and a window overlooking the bay. Fields of granite and hardship in all directions, the band was hot, the bass guitar blending with the bodhran, a girl in her twenties belting out "She Moves Through the Fair" and the whole evening jelled. Tommy, the other side of three hot ones, asked,

"You hear about the guy who walked."

He indicated the ocean, added,

"Out there."

I was mellow, a nice buzz building, the music, the fire. Giving me the illusion of peace, I asked,

"This like a true story?"

"You care, the fuck it matters?"

He had a point, I didn't care, this stage of the evening, it was a time for tales. Veracity didn't register on the radar. A little testy, he went,

"You want to hear it or not?"

"Go for it."

He knocked back most of his hot one, a clove caught in his tooth, he said,

"Fucking things, ruin a decent whiskey."

Then,

"Some guy, who lived near here, single, with lots of land, the ceili on a Saturday night."

I said,

"Living it large."

"Shut up. Seems he had inoperable cancer, so he goes down to the beach."

Tommy looked out at the wild horizon, pointed,

"Over there a ways. Wearing his best suit and get this . . . Wellingtons."

I couldn't help it, said,

"No outfit complete without them."

Tommy signalled for another round, the band had launched into "I Never Will Marry" as if they knew the story. One of those odd moments of serendipity. Tommy said,

"There's a point here and I'll eventually make it. The guy, he loads his pockets with stones and the Wellingtons."

Tommy's on his feet now, moving his legs sluggishly, attempting to walk, the stones weighing him down, continues,

"The guy can hardly move but he manages to wade in the water, fighting the current, the fucker is determined, these Connemara men, they're warriors, bro, and eventually, gets to where he's under the water. Can you see it, Steve?"

"Jesus, not sure I want to."

The drinks came, clouds rising from the hot glasses, brown sugar melting on the bottoms, black pints riding point. I gave the guy a bunch of notes, he's staring at Tommy, who's gasping for breath, the water in his mouth, strangling his lungs, his eyes closed, he says,

"And he's standing on the bottom, weighed down but

upright because of the stones and he drowns, facing out."

Tommy opened his eyes, sweat on his forehead and I go,
"Some story."

He selects a fresh pint, inspects the head, then takes a
sip, says,
"He left a note."

"Aw, come on!"

Tommy looks offended, then,
"It was in the paper. The guy said he wanted to be a sentinel, standing there forever, facing America."

My mood was ebbing so I tried,
"Well, god knows, he was dressed for it."

Tommy was staring at the ocean, said,
"He's out there, looking to America, waiting."

The band took a break, headed to the bar so I asked,
"Waiting for what?"

Tommy pulled his eyes back to me, was silent, then,
"Godot, fuck's sakes, you don't get it, do you?"

"What's to get?"

He drained the pint, up, swallow, down, one motion,
then,
"You need an explanation, it's gone, forget it."

End of the evening, the band, finished with Christy
Moore's "Ride On." The girl sang it with such yearning,
such loss that I felt a lump in my throat. We got outside,
waiting for a cab, the night air hit us like a banshee, cata-
pulting us into another level of intoxication. I pointed at
the coast, said,
"You're thinking of him, the sentinel, out there."

And got that look from him, he was five years old again,
he said,

"Fuck no, I'm thinking of fish and chips."

Me, I'm Irish, I love music. I'm a huge fan of Springsteen. "Meeting Across the River," I played that track for Tommy once, he goes,

"Shit, again."

Three more times, he's mouthing the lyrics, then says, his version of the line,

"Could be you're carrying a mate."

STAPLETON HAD PROCURED three Irish army uniforms, we were in a rented apartment in Salthill, at the rear of the building. You couldn't see the bay. I asked Tommy,

"Why'd you get *a room without a view*, what's that about?"

Tommy shrugged.

"Fucked if I know."

Then I heard,

"I don't do views."

Stapleton had emerged from a bedroom, a characteristic of his, just appearing suddenly. The original stealth bomber. The uniforms lay on a couch, Stapleton said,

"Try one."

He was dressed in black T-shirt, black combat trousers, bare feet, his arms were a riot of botched tattoos, as if the ink ran out. Prison jobs. I asked,

"And if it doesn't fit, I'll what, get it altered?"

He smiled, like he could be a fun guy, shoot the shit, asked,

"The Free State Army, you hear of them being commended for their tailoring?"

Northerners!

The Republic is always the Free State, lest you ever forget their agenda. I tried on the uniform, the tunic was tight and the trousers too long. He said,

"You'll be armed, that's what people focus on."

I took it off and he added,

"Can't wait to get out of it, you more comfortable with the British one?"

Tommy intervened:

"Whoa, guys, lighten up, we've a lot of stuff to cover."

And to chill me, adds the line from the Springsteen song, changing it a bit:

"Gotta remember not to smile."

We didn't have a lot of stuff to cover, nor did we lighten up. The plan was almost beautiful in its simplicity. After we'd been through it a few times, Tommy asked,

"Seem okay to you, Steve?"

Stapleton said,

"It is okay."

I looked over at the uniforms, said,

"I see Sergeant's stripes, let me guess, it's not Tommy and we can be certain it's not me."

Stapleton faced me, asked,

"You have a problem taking orders, son?"

I laughed out loud, echoed,

"*Son*, Jesus, what are you, my old man? My problem is taking orders from you."

Tommy again:

"Steve, it's cool, he's done it lots of times."

I waved a hand at him, said,

"Butt out."

Stapleton began a series of flexing exercises, said,

"You and me, son, this job is done, we'll have a wee chat, how does that sound?"

"Sounds perfect."

Tommy produced a six-pack, asked,

"Who's for a brew?"

No takers, so he had one himself, Stapleton asked,

"You know how to handle a SIG?"

"Yeah."

"That's what you'll be carrying."

And he strolled back to the bedroom. Tommy was on his second beer, said,

"He's not so bad, Steve."

I let it hover then.

"You really believe that?"

He opened another can, said,

"A few more of these, I'll believe anything."

Before I left, he said,

"I was watching *The Simpsons* last night."

"So?"

"Bleeding Gums, the musician, was teaching Lisa to play the blues."

"Wow, Tommy, the shitstorm we're in, I'm glad you get to relax."

He ignored my tone, he was talking to himself,

"Lisa says she doesn't feel any better after playing."

I was with Lisa on that note and Tommy says,

"Gums explains the blues isn't about you feeling better, it's about making others feel worse."

I waited but that was it. I asked,

"That's it, that's the point?"

And he laughed, spluttering suds, goes,

"That's the beauty, there is no point."

He was tanked, mutilating the Springsteen line,

"Change your clothes 'cos we're like, having us an encounter."

I slammed the door on my way out.

Walking along the Salthill Promenade, rain was coming in over the bay and I turned my face into it. What was I hoping, some symbolic washing clean? Behind me was my best friend, guzzling beer at 11:30 in the morning, talking shite.

A paramilitary psycho, just itching to take me apart, bogus army uniforms thrown on a sofa.

Jesus.

All the years of laughter with Tommy, all flushed down the toilet. The oddest thing, I remembered what Patrick Moynihan said when John F. Kennedy was killed. A woman had said to him, *We'll never laugh again*. He answered, *Oh, we'll laugh again, it's just we'll never be young again*.

The light rain became a torrent.

Siobhan only ever got one look at Stapleton, said,

"He's the devil."

I warned Tommy,

"You keep him away from Siobhan, away from my home."

It was two days later and he had his hair cut to the bone, should as the Irish say *have taken years off him.*

It didn't.

He said,

"Stapleton gets in your life, he's all over it, like a virus."

I moved my hand, grabbed Tommy by the shoulder, said,

"I'm serious, you keep that snake out of my life."

And more Springsteen, man, was I sorry I'd played him the song.

"Bro, we gotta stay mellow as we're way out on a limb."

It annoyed the hell out of me that he never quoted the lines correctly, always bent them to his own tone.

It was four days to the bank job, I'd brought Tommy to my place, tried to get some food into his system. Siobhan had left a pot of stew and I piled a plate with that, added some extra spuds and meat, put it before him, said,

"Yo, partner, time to chow down."

He brightened for a moment then,

"Partner! You think that, Steve? I'm like your buddy?"

Striving for some semblance of sanity, I'd poured glasses of milk.

Jeez, what was I thinking?

Raised mine, said,

"You need to ask, 'course you are, always have been, Slainte amach (cheers with good feeling)."

He looked at the milk as if he'd never seen such a product before, asked,

"Got any beer?"

Determined or nuts or both, I said,

"Get that down, you, line your stomach."

The phone rang and I went to answer it. The music shop, was I coming back to work, like, anytime soon?

Nope.

I returned to the table and Tommy was putting something in his pocket, saw a glint of silver, for a mad moment I thought he was stealing the cutlery or worse, he was carrying. He gave me a huge smile, said,

"See, Dad, I finished all my milk."

Later, when I was piling the stuff in the sink, his glass reeked of whiskey.

I wanted to kill him, actually muttered aloud,

"You bollix, I could happily wring your neck."

That muttering would be just one more thing to lash and lambaste myself with.

That night in bed with Siobhan, she asked,

"What's happening?"

I didn't lie much to her as a rule. She'd grown up in an abusive home, had a low threshold for lies. Her father, a wife beater, had shattered most of her illusions. Money to her was the only freedom, you got enough, you got away. If not clean, at least untainted.

I told her.

Her brother had done time for burglary, so I didn't have any high moral ground to negotiate. She asked,

"How dangerous is it?"

I wanted to believe we'd covered the angles but when weapons are present, scratch that. I said,

"The most dangerous element is Stapleton."

She'd only seen Tommy twice since his homecoming and he'd been cordial if distant. She said,

"Tommy is the danger, he's like a junkie with the beginnings of withdrawal."

I didn't see a whole lot of mileage in disputing that, said,

"Well, he's certainly got enough dope to see him through."

She'd been resting her head on my chest, pulled back, said,

"Not withdrawal from drugs, he's withdrawing from life, gone but to wash him."

I hadn't heard that expression in a long time. A person on their death bed, they receive a final cleansing, the moments before the close. I said,

"I'll watch his back, don't worry."

She turned on her side, fixed the pillow, asked,

"I'm not worried about him. Who'll watch your back?"

LOATH AS I AM to admit it, Stapleton knew his craft. The bank was in the centre of Shop Street. Four streets converged at its location, he'd planted smoke bombs in five premises nearby, designed to go off with maximum volume. We had three cars for the task. Move and change. Keep moving, keep changing, never let them fix on a definite vehicle. Over and over, like a mantra, he intoned it.

Made sense.

We were sitting in the first car, uncomfortable in the uniforms. Watched as the army stood outside the bank, the bags of money being carried from the trucks. I was in the front with Stapleton, the assault rifle between my knees, barrel to the floor. Stapleton was sliding the rack on a Browning automatic. Tommy, in back, was singing quietly. Stapleton barked,

"Cut that out."

Tommy nodded and Stapleton added,

"Adjust your beret, soldier, it's crooked."

He glanced at me, I asked,

"Getting antsy there, fellah?"

And got the look, he said,

"I don't get antsy, I get the job done."

Then the first bomb went, sounding loud and lethal. Tommy moved and Stapleton gritted.

"Steady."

Then, in rapid succession, three more, the smoke began to cloud the street, Stapleton rooted in a hold-all, took out the canisters, said,

"Let's roll."

The soldiers had begun to disperse up the street. We were out and Stapleton lobbed the CS . . . We pulled on the gas masks, chaos on the make. We got into the bank, pulled off the masks, then into the centre. Two soldiers, confused, were standing by the money, Stapleton barked,

"You two, secure the rear."

They hesitated and I knew he'd take them down, then they registered his stripes and moved off. We lifted the bags and Stapleton shouted at the staff,

"Keep your heads down."

They did.

I couldn't believe how smooth it was going. Glanced at Tommy, sweat on his forehead, his eyes dancing in his head, he muttered,

"This fucking rocks."

He was electric, cranked on the action. We got to the door, a guard there. Stapleton said,

"Officer, ensure the staff remain inside."

The tone of command, air of authority, it's awesome.

The guard near ran to his assignment, I swear I saw a tiny smile light the corner of Stapleton's mouth. We were down the street, that close to a clean job when it fell apart. Threw the money in the boot and heard,

"Don't move."

A young soldier, his rifle cocked, had approached from nowhere, Tommy panicked, lifted his weapon, and the soldier let off a burst, more from nerves than intent. His face shocked as the rounds tore into Tommy's chest. Stapleton turned, shot the soldier in the head, said,

"Go, go, go!"

Pulled Tommy in the back, Stapleton jumped in beside him. I got behind the wheel, reversed, got out into Mary Street, pulled off my tunic and cap, a shirt and tie beneath.

Citizen.

Drove to the Square. Despite all my inclinations, I kept to the speed limit. Stapleton was lying over Tommy, you couldn't see them from outside, I asked,

"How's he doing?

"Shut up, drive."

At Salthill, I pulled in behind the large, empty ballroom, our second car was there. Transferred Tommy to that, he looked bad. Three minutes, I was driving along the promenade, driving slowly, I could hear sirens all the way. They wouldn't be looking for a single man, in a suit, driving leisurely by the bay. The third car was outside Spiddal, down a boreen. This is Irish for a road that defies description. I pulled up, got out carefully, a deep ridge on my left, almost a precipice. We'd selected it to dump the uniforms. Stapleton got out, said,

"He's not going to make it."

"The fuck you know, we've got to get help."

He was shaking his head, said,

"I've seen gunshot wounds, there's no return from this one, and if he recovered, what, the rest of his life in jail?"

Before I could answer, he turned, put two bullets in Tommy's face, then the gun moving up. I had the rifle, slammed him between the eyes with the stock. He gave a tiny o, then fell backwards, crashed down the precipice, was lost from view. I should have followed, put one in the back of his skull.

"Once you get a feeling for handling nitroglycerine fuses, you never lose it."

— HUNTER S. THOMPSON, "Kingdom of Fear"

I WAS IN A CAB, had told the driver to take me to the East Village, and as it did, the vision rose up before my eyes:

Tommy's broken body, his ruined face. I'd carried him to the water's edge, fucking tears coursing down my cheeks, muttering,

"I'm not going to weep."

Weighed him with stones, their weight as heavy as the lash upon my heart. Then, barely able to hold him, laden with the rocks, I waded into the water. The current pulled at us and the cold, my body going numb. Got as far as chest level, then let him go, said,

"Join your sentinel, *mi amigo.*"

In Irish, there is a lament, torn from centuries of poverty, oppression, violence. It goes . . .

"Och ocon."

Hard to render the exact meaning, but *woe is me* comes close. Or, fuck this.

We Irish have the lock on melancholy, never happier

than when we're sad, rising to our finest moments on prayers of lamentation. Our best music, best writing has at its core a profound sense of grief. We've never been short of reasons why and the rain doesn't help.

Bronach.

I love that word, the sound of it, literally it's sadness but a step beyond, the place where you are broken. I shook myself, had to move out of the shadows, rid myself of spectres. If Galway had been absolute sadness, then let New York be about survival. I rolled the window down, let the sound of the city drown out the Irish echoes.

The cabbie asked,

"What about them Cubs?"

Treating me like I'd know, I wasn't going to blow it, said,

"Man, isn't that something?"

He bought it, energised, continued:

"The goddamn play-offs, first time in eighty-seven years, what a blast."

He went into a long rap about the history and I finally gathered they came out of Chicago, am I quick or what? Tommy those last days, said,

"Tell you what, Steve, when I tire of New York, I'm getting my ass up to the Windy City."

I was surprised, Irish people, eager to escape the damp, don't plan on moving from one city of harsh winter to one that's even worse; I asked,

"Don't you want sun, to never see rain again?"

With the drugs, booze, Stapleton, the impending robbery, we hadn't been easy with each other. For that brief interlude, our friendship was restored and he was animated, said in a near perfect American tone,

"Chicago is the hog butcher, it's *the* American city. New York is like Hong Kong, limey and chink but then really neither. What I'm going to do, bro—"

He hadn't called me that in a long time, it gave me the most treacherous of feelings, it gave me hope, he continued:

"—is get us into a really good hotel in Lincoln Park. We don't want to be downtown, fuck that, we're not tourists, you ever read anything about the city?"

I hadn't.

"I'll take you on a tour of the real Chicago. Forget Michigan Avenue, the shops and shit, we're going to party, I'll buy you a beer in Algren's Rainbow Club at Damen and Division, I'll show you county jail . . ."

He paused, sparks in his eyes, seeing it, seeing us, free and coasting. The buddy system in extremis. More . . .

"We'll smoke a joint by Chicago's PD and yes, we cannot forget a cappuccino on Tiger Street, in memory of Sam Giacana and Tony "Joe Batters" Accardo. Then up to Grand Avenue for an Italian beef at Salerno's so we can talk to the ghosts of the Spilottro brothers. Hey, jeez, if the Bulls are in town, we might catch a game, what do you say, Steve, sound like something you can get your head round?"

What it sounded was great, I could almost see it, too, asked,

"How the hell do you know so much about Chicago?"

And the momentum began to leak away, I could see the light slowly draining from his eyes, creeping back into darkness, he said,

"I'm just blowing smoke, probably be too cold for you."

I wanted him back, full of vim and devilment, tried,

"No, Tommy, sounds great, we'll do it."

And then he turned his head, the distant drummer was near, looked right at me, said,

"Truth is, Steve, you're not a Chicago kind of guy."

That hurt, like, a lot, and I'm still not fully sure I understood the meaning of what he said. I do know it was a farewell and it shut me down, shut me out . . . och ocon. Times, I'd hear his voice, especially if he was on the Chicago rap.

Like this.

"We will destroy the Florida Marlins at Wrigley Field. They will die horribly and (worse), without honour although if any team needs to be smote "without honour" it is the New York Yankees. Plus, I hope New York beats Boston like they do every year—the Boston Red Sox cry and cry and always fuck up when they get the chance for the series. But the Cubs, man, they've gotta win."

Jesus. Tommy, like so many other things got that hopelessly wrong, the Red Sox took the World Series.

The cabbie was calling me,

"Yo, buddy, time to wake up and smell the coffee."

Yeah.

I paid him, laid the mandatory five on top. He said,

"Have a good one."

There's a music store in the East Village that specialises in vintage stuff; the last thing I wanted to do was listen to music but I figured, if I ordered Siobhan's favourites, she'd be delighted when she got to Tucson and found them waiting. The guy behind the counter was friendly, opened,

"Irish, right?"

Lotta work to do on that accent.

I ordered Planxty, Rory Gallagher, Clannad, The Saw Doctors. The guy was nodding, liked the selection, and I asked,

"Can you ship them to Tucson?"

He was a New Yorker, he could ship them to China. I gave the address of the Lazy 8 in Tucson and his interest perked, he said,

"That's like a dude ranch."

I agreed and then he asked,

"You mind me asking? What's with Tucson, what's that about?"

I had to smile, Americans, right up front, they'll ask you your business, and they know you, maybe, all of five minutes.

In Ireland, you know someone for years, and I mean years, and still, you're hesitant to ask them the exact nature of their life. I said, only half kidding,

"Always wanted to be a cowboy."

He took my credit card, did the deal, then, as I left he cautioned

"Watch for them sidewinders."

The rest of the day, I walked the city. In my head was Aimee Mann, jeez, when had I listened to her? Where did she spring from, unless her songs of guilt were related to my shame, my agony at the callous betrayal of Siobhan.

She remains among the great underrated, the true unappreciated. As Tommy often said.

"Fuck, she rocks."

Ain't that the truth.

*　　*　　*

On pure impulse, I called Kaitlin, Siobhan had given me her number, said,

"If you get a chance, give her a call, see how she's doing, she'd love to see you."

Wasn't so sure how smart it was, she was intuitive or maybe I was just guilty but would she spot I'd been, what's the word, unfaithful? Women have this sense of betrayal, maybe because they're so accustomed to it. Rang the number, her apartment number, and hoped I'd get the answering service, then my duty would be done and I'd say, what, *sorry I missed you. Pity we couldn't have got together, maybe when Siobhan arrives.*

She answered her own self and was thrilled to hear me. Her day off, talk about poor timing. Arranged to meet her for lunch on Lexington in two hours, she ended with,

"Dying to hear all your news."

Jesus.

I was standing outside the restaurant she'd selected in plenty of time, get my face composed to hide the lying I'd been doing. A slender woman stopped, smiled, and I did a double take, croaked,

"Kaitlin?"

She'd lost a ton of weight, her hair was cut short, and she was dressed in casual but expensive jeans and trainers. A soft suede jacket that roared *money* draped on her arm. She held out her arms, asked,

"I don't get a hug?"

She did.

We went into the restaurant and a line was already formed, I said,

"Shit."

Kaitlin laughed, said,

"I booked."

We were escorted to a table, seated, and I marvelled at the change in her. Before I could ask, she said,

"Atkins."

I shook my head, went,

"Miraculous."

And meant it, it wasn't just the weight she'd lost, though that was startling enough, it was her whole demeanour, she had a whole poised confidence. A waiter took our drinks order, sparkling water for her, Miller for me. Kaitlin had been plagued with bad skin, not unrelated to the greasy food she'd such a liking for. Siobhan had told me that she fretted constantly, had tried everything to clear it.

Now, her skin was luminous, shining in its health. She touched her face, wonder in her eyes, said,

"I've even new skin."

What I was trying to achieve. I said,

"You're transformed."

We ordered steaks, lean, and nothing else for her, with fries and all the lashings for me. She studied me, said,

"You look tired."

Whoops.

I sighed, went with the,

"New city, takes a time."

She laughed, said,

"Tell me about it."

Jeez, she even sounded American with the Irish lilt just coasting beneath. The food arrived and between bites, she told me about her job, a promotion already, her apartment, cramped but close to work, and a guy she was seeing. He was, she said, something in the city, meaning, lots of bucks and though a little bland, he was good to her. She used the throwaway line of dismissal,

"He'll do."

Till somebody more exciting came along, she obviously registered my expression and asked,

"You think that's mercenary?"

I did, but hell, was I going to admit it, nope. She launched,

"What you and Siobhan have, you think that's common, it's so rare as to be nonexistent and where is she, what the devil are you doing here on your own?"

I gave her the song and dance about me getting everything settled, having all arranged. She didn't believe a word of it, said in complete American,

"What a crock."

I gave a last lustre defence but she shook her head, said,

"There's something you're not telling me but I won't push it, all I ask is you don't screw her around."

The word *screw* causing me more than a moment's fright. Then a thought hit her and she asked,

"Your surname, Blake, didn't you guys used to be Prods?"

I kept my tone light, said,

"A long time ago."

Now she was completely Irish:

"Ary, them crowd, they never change."

Before I could argue, if argument there is, she asked,

"What about that creature, that demon who follows you around, what rock is he hiding under?"

Tommy.

If I'd said,

"Under the whole of the Atlantic Ocean,"

Would she have felt bad? I don't think so, and she definitely wouldn't have been surprised. I said he hadn't made this trip and she didn't respond. We were finished with the meal and she declined coffee or anything else. I called for the cheque and she protested but not too strongly. Outside, she immediately lit a cigarette and I was astonished, she looked at me, went,

"What?"

"You're smoking."

A flush of anger hit her cheeks and she said,

"You think a complete transformation like I've achieved is without price, you live here, it's stressful."

She suddenly looked on the verge of tears, said,

"I miss home."

And I said,

"Go home."

She ground the cig under her expensive trainers with a ferocity, vowed,

"Not if it was my dying wish."

I hugged her and she whispered,

"Mind that girl, she's priceless."

I promised and said I'd call her soon.

For a moment she looked up the sky, seeing what, I don't know, Galway Bay, the pubs of the town, and then she said,

"You have a cold spot, Steve, you probably can't help it,

but Siobhan, she lights you up, try not to be the usual gobshite and fuck it up."

I wanted to part from her with a lightness, to leave with
a good feeling and asked,

"You think I'm a gobshite."

She stared right into my face, said,

"You're a man, it's your nature."

Got back to the hotel, tired, recognised the limo outside.
Juan's driver, smoking, leaning against the hood, I was
tempted to pun,

"Boy on the hood."

Maybe not.

He clocked me, flicked the cig, and rapped the glass of
the back window. Juan peered out, said,

"Bro, need you."

I sure as fuck didn't need him, I was sick to death of him,
said,

"Not now."

Juan was wearing a pale leather jacket, Calvin Klein
jeans, Bally loafers, designer git.

He looked at the driver, an expression passing between
them, hard to decipher but warmth was not on its agenda.
Juan smiled, a new gold molar gleaming, said,

"I'm in a jam here, bro, you gonna diss me?"

Diss, fuck.

I was seriously tired but said,

"Okay, but can we get to it, I'm like, beat."

He nodded and the driver relaxed, I slid in beside Juan,
his cologne overpowering, he slapped my knee, went,

"*Muchas gracias, amigo.*"

He leaned over to a briefcase, opened it, took out a cellophane bag, the white powder heavy in its weight, began to roll a line on the cover of the case, asked,

"Hit you?"

"No thanks."

He raised an eyebrow, mocking,

"Set you right up, bro."

I shook my head. He did two fat ones, then went into that snorting, nose pulling, wheezing they do. What it is, is fucking annoying. Finally, he leaned his head back, went,

"Ah, *Dios mio*, here comes the ice."

He uttered little sighs of near-orgasm then sat bolt upright. Pulled the leather jacket aside, asked,

"You know what this is, bro?"

It was a gun, a big one, I said,

"Looks uncomfortable is what it is, you ask me."

He laughed, then in bullet Spanish, repeated my hilarity to the driver. He, not a fun guy like Juan, just grunted. Juan said,

"Ramon no like you."

Gee.

I stared straight ahead, deadpanned,

"What a shame."

Juan used his index finger to tap the gun's butt, said,

"This a Walther PPK 3805 automatic, like them CIA dudes got themselves."

What was I to say . . . congratulations? Went,

"And you need it for?

Gave me an evil smile. There's a line in the Johnny Cash song about a guy going round taking names.

Always seemed threatening to me and seemed appropriate for whatever direction this conversation was headed. We arrived at Clinton Street, another song, Leonard Cohen, another heartbeat. We got out and Juan indicated a building on the other side of the street, said,

"Ees my office."

Heavy on the "*ees.*" Ramon fucked off with the limo, I'd miss him. Juan had a shitpile of keys, got various locks opened and we were in, got an elevator to the third floor, Juan was a ball of energy, all of it strung. His fingers clicking, foot tapping, a tic below his left eye, I was tempted to ask,

"You ever audition for Riverdance?"

Then into the office, two large rooms, with leather furniture, massive TV, and box upon box of electronic equipment. Juan indicated I should sit down so I did, in a leather armchair, the fabric creaking as I sat. Juan moved to a cabinet, pulled open the door. Bottles of booze, every brand you could imagine. He got two glasses, then kicked a mini fridge, shovelled some ice in the glasses, held up a bottle, asked,

"Tequila good for you, *mi amigo*?"

I could be wrong but I swear it had the worm in the bottom or was that Juan? I asked,

"Got seven and seven?"

I was John Cheever in the flesh, the suburban ideal, Juan squinted, went,

"*Qué?*"

"Segram's and 7UP."

It pissed him off, he held up the tequila like some holy relic, asked,

"You no like my country's drink?"

The phony accent was getting on my nerves, urging me to go,

"The Bronx is a country?"

Yeah, drop that into the already loaded atmosphere, see how it jelled. I settled for Wild Turkey, on the rocks. Juan had his back to me as I took a sip, then he turned, the Walther in his hand, said,

"You cocksucker, you put the meat to my old lady."

I **NOTICED** a slight tremor in his hand and that was a worry. His finger could squeeze involuntarily. I stood up, the leather protesting, Juan shouted,

"I tell you to move, motherfucker?"

The drink was in my left hand, carefully, no sudden movement, I put it on one of the boxes, asked,

"You ever read James Lee Burke?"

"What?"

"Or Andrew Vachss, you read at all?"

The barrel was moving left to right, spittle at the corner of Juan's mouth, he wanted to use it, asked,

"The fuck you talking about?"

I sighed, explained,

"Great writers, thing is, they both have an expression for a guy like you."

His tongue was darting in and out of his mouth, like a

Galway eel, slippery, wet, and mainly repugnant, he was explosive, shouted,

"Like me, they know me, they put names on me, I put a cap in their heads."

I stayed absolutely still, my whole body language presenting no threat, said,

"Burke calls you a meltdown, and Vachss, he'd have you down as skel."

He didn't get the meaning but he sure as hell got the implication. As the insult registered, it was time to act. The British army, in training, they beat you up, vomit you out. One of the very first lessons you learn is how to disarm a man. Vital if you're headed for the streets of the Ardoyne. It's an action so simple, so beautiful, it's close to art.

Right foot forward, pressure on the left, palm of the right hand fast and straight, left zooming in to slap the gunman's head as his weapon sails above his head. Here's the best bit, you allow him a moment to wonder,

"What the fuck just happened?"

And as he begins to ask, "How'd he do that?" You give him a ferocious kick in the balls.

Add,

"Don't ever point a gun at me."

That's the macho bit.

On the Plains of Salisbury, a desolate acre of desperation, a thousand times I'd be put through that routine. Most nights I went to bed, I could hardly breathe because of the pain in my balls. Teach a man through his genitalia, he's a real fast study.

Juan was writhing on the floor, a litany of Spanish prayers leaking from his mouth. Usually as the groin pain recedes, you break the nose or two fingers, keep them focused, but I wasn't flashy. Picked up the gun and my drink, sat on the edge of the table, said,

"The way that leather creaks, it's a bastard to sit in."

He fixed his eyes on me, hatred like the proverbial coals, tried to speak but hurting, his manhood in his throat, a gargle was the best he could manage.

He gargled.

I was tapping the barrel of the gun on the rim of the glass, an irritating sound, said,

"We've got us, what you gangbangers call, let me see, yeah, a situation."

I hadn't decided on whether to kill him but I was giving it some consideration. Maybe meant two for one as I'd probably have to off Ramon, too. His vocal cords were finding a level and he tried,

"You going to *keel* me, you think you have the *cojones*?"

Credit to him, he dragged up some saliva, with a massive effort, spat, not a whole bunch but it reached the floor, so I shot him.

Gut shot first. Get the serious pain started, raised the sights, aiming at his Adam's apple, saw a British army colonel demonstrate that one time. Takes the apple right out the back of the neck. He'd used colour slides to show the aftereffect, looks like you took a combine harvester to it. Juan was in too much pain to grasp the story.

Changed my mind.

Stood up, said,

"You keep it in your pants *amigo*."

Out on the street, before anything else, I dumped the

gun in a grate then hailed a cab. At the hotel, I moved fast, got my gear packed, then down to the desk, the clerk, surprised, asked,

"You're leaving us, Mr. Blake?"

"You got it."

As he booted up the screen, he persisted,

"Was everything to your satisfaction?"

I acted like I had to think about it, then,

"Hunky dory."

He smiled, said,

"David Bowie, right?"

"Yeah, whatever."

Another cab. My mind locked down, locked tight. So much for plans, I'd wanted to stay in New York longer, reimmerse myself in the way of life. Not that America is New York, but as a launching pad, it's pretty good. Get that dialogue down, ensure the smooth transaction of the money through Siobhan. And take a block of time to grieve for Tommy. I was never going to get over him but had hoped I'd find a level of acceptance.

What'd I do?

Shot the one friend he had.

Nice going, Steve-o.

The driver asked,

"What airline, buddy?"

I said the first thing came into my head:

"American."

He launched into a rap about Iraq, about farmboys from Iowa and the heartland. Kids, he called them, dying every day in the rebuilding of that forsaken country. We got to the airport and as I reached for my wallet, he asked,

"So, what do you think of my solution?"

I'd never heard it, tuned out as I was, so I said, laying a ten on the fare,

"Can't see how it would fail."

He gave me a suspicious look but all he got was my neutral face, tried,

"The Jets choked, huh?"

Let him see I was a player but the wrong guy, he near spat, went,

"I follow hockey, them Bruins, outta Boston, that's a game."

Juan in the limo, between lines of coke had lectured me on American sport, said,

"Hockey is for bitches."

I didn't think I'd share this with the cabbie, so I said,

"You better believe it buddy."

And he was gone. A valet asked if I needed help and I wanted to go,

"Do I ever?"

But waved him off, I found the ticket desk and the clerk asked,

"Where you headed?"

"When's the next flight to Vegas?"

Why not. I was already on the biggest gamble of my life. He said,

"You're in luck."

And I nearly smiled, a flight was leaving in forty minutes, I said that'd be good and he asked,

"Round trip?"

"One way."

Didn't faze him and he punched out my ticket. Almost a

pun there, I'd just punched Juan's ticket. I paid by credit card, always the anxious moment. Was Siobhan as good as she claimed, was the money going through as smooth as she promised, he handed me a pen, asked,

"Sign here, please."

I did.

Siobhan was on the money.

Security was even tighter on domestic flights. I joined a line of shoeless people, a man in front, turned, looked at me, said,

"You're going to have to remove those, buddy."

I nodded, took off my loafers, put my change, watch in my jacket, took that off, bundled them in a tray. The security people were grim-faced but kept the line moving, a woman protested,

"I've got film in here."

The guard, patient, said,

"Then take it out."

She started to complain, saying she was the mother of four grown kids, did she look like some . . . like . . . terrorist? Even I knew she was buying grief. Sure enough, after she stepped through the metal detector, she was herded to one side, given the full treatment. First, stretch out her arms, the hand detector all over her body, then, "take a seat, Ma'am." The loaded politeness in the address, the easy intimidation through manners and then, raise her right leg, then the left. All done with deliberate slowness, my turn and as I stepped to the base, ZING. The guy said,

"Step back, sir."

I did, was asked if I'd any other metal on my person, I touched my neck, said,

"A medal."

The guy nodded, motioned me through, he asked,

"That Saint Christopher?"

"No, it's the Miraculous Medal."

He stared at me, said,

"Irish, huh?"

"Yes, sir."

Bounce them manners right back, he said,

"That's like a talisman, a good luck deal, right?"

Did I want to make a convert, explain the significance of the Mother of God? I settled for,

"She keeps us safe."

And got a tired smile, he was in the security business, at the literal hands on end of the business, he said,

"Man needs all the protection he can get."

Argue that.

I was going to say, a Walther PPK doesn't hurt either, but you don't mention weapons to those guys, especially when you're almost clear, so I asked,

"You get a lot of hassle in your work?"

He rolled his eyes, like *tell me about it*, said,

"Some. The way it is, some folks get real uptight, but me, it's my job, do it right."

He was waving me by, added,

"What we do, they get difficult, we go real slooowww...."

And winked, then,

"They move fast or slow, ain't never no mind to me, I get paid by the hour, not the passenger."

The American work ethic right there. The job gets done. Then he was calling the next passenger. Manners might not make the man but they sure as hell smooth the passage. I went to Starbucks, got a tall latte, added a little vanilla, get those flavours blending, then looked round the airport, most everyone had a coffee in hand, a caffeined world. No wonder the planet was jittery. I'd some time yet, headed straight for the music outlet, bought a Gretchen Peters CD, the new one, *Halcyon*, strapped on my headphones.

I got a seat near my gate, took a sip of the latte, began to listen to Gretchen, she soothes my soul. A track from years ago, what first got me tuned to her . . . "On a Bus to St. Cloud." Such longing in the lyrics and, too, the awful loss that never goes away.

My flight was boarding.

Bhi curamach . . . Be careful

I GOT MY SEAT, the aisle of course. The window was taken by an obese man. Bulging over the small space, the seat belt like a bad girdle, barely containing him. He was wearing a Hawaiian shirt like the squad in Jack Lord's outfit, sweat was already climbing under his arms, I nearly went,

"O-la."

He gave a sheepish grin, said,

"Guess I should have booked two seats, you think?"

I thought he needed to cut out the burgers, but smiled noncommitedly. He extended a fat hand.

"Bob Milovitz, outta Chicago."

His hand was drenched in perspiration and did I want to touch it, like fuck, took it, said,

"Stephen Blake."

Wanted to add the rider,

"Outta my depth."

He gave a huge grin, delighted, asked,

"Irish, yeah?"

"Yes."

He went into the near mandatory American reply:

"I got me some Irish on my mom's side, third generation then Polack on Granddaddy's, even some Scottish Presbyterian."

The Americans present themselves like a cocktail, a mix of genetic influences, delivered with pride.

U2, pride in the name of love or whatever.

He gave me a quizzical look, asked,

"You in the services?"

Came out of left field, I faltered, went,

"Excuse me?"

His brow was awash in sweat, rivulets coursing down his swollen jowls. Thing is, I liked him. Not knowing one item about him, intuition told me he was a decent man, and like, how many of those do you meet? In my forty years, I met maybe three. Was it worth the wait? I do know it's so rare, you recognise the quality straight off.

There's a lighthouse off Galway Bay, the beacon is erratic, sweeps the water at the most unexpected moments. When it does, your spirits are lifted, especially if it happens obliquely. He apologised,

"Don't mean to pry."

I thought, then why are you doing it? He continued,

"But hey, we're on our way to Vegas, where truth is the flip of a card but you sit like an army brat. You mightn't believe it but I was in the corps, did a hitch at Fort Bragg."

And he laughed, a deep rumble, continued,

"Yeah, catering, as you can see, thing is, I recognise other vets, they never lose that bearing."

As I said, I liked him, so I conceded,

"Yeah, I did a jolt."

"In these here United States?"

Since 9/11, the dignity ordinary joes imbue that term with, he had it in bucketfuls. I said,

"No, another man's army."

I wasn't prepared to give any more. He gave a rueful grin, said,

"Same deal, am I right?"

I was saved a reply by the engines rumbling. He said,

"Man, I hate flying."

We didn't talk till after takeoff, the plane levelled out and the seat belt sign clicked off. Bob asked,

"Any sign of the drinks cart?"

I looked round, said,

"Any minute now."

Fifteen minutes later, it came. He ordered a Bloody Mary and I opted for Maker's Mark. Bob said,

"You know your hooch."

We hit a blast of turbulence and the plane veered, put the shite crossways in me, Bob went pale, muttered,

"Uh-oh."

I was with him on that. Five more minutes of lurching and diving, I'd downed the bourbon in one. Bob's glass was empty, too, I said,

"They've suspended the trolley service."

He'd gone paler, staring straight ahead, he asked,

"Wanna get drunk?"

Without moving his head, he pointed down, said,

"My carry-on, could you reach it?"

I could. He said,

"Open it."

Jesus, I remembered Juan, in the limo, the first time, nudging a briefcase, saying those exact words.

No guns here but maybe as lethal, stacks of miniatures, every brand. He gave a sheepish grin, said,

"I collect 'em."

I selected seven: three vodka, two Easy Times, two rum.

Got the vodka in his glass, I drank the bourbon from the tiny bottle, drank fast. The turbulence eased and Bob uncapped a few more. In jig time, I'd a nice buzz building, Bob asked,

"Where you staying in Vegas?"

I'd no idea, said,

"I've no idea."

He laughed, said,

"I'm at the Sahara, for the poker."

I nodded as if this made sense. The hostess came by, saw the mess of little bottles, asked,

"Party time, guys?"

Bob asked,

"Got any pretzels, nuts?"

She gave a winning smile, said,

"We'll be serving dinner soon but I'll see what we've got."

She looked at me and I went,

"No nuts."

Came off as,

"Numb nuts."

Sent Bob into the giggles. He said in that way Americans have,

"I like you, buddy."

It's so forthright. So almost innocent.

I come from a completely different race. We'd near die before we'd say such a thing. Tommy was my best friend, we'd be through hell and high water, spent an inordinate amount of time together and the closest we'd ever come to such a statement was,

"Ah, you're not the worst."

And even that is couched in throwaway style, lest it sound too intimate, too invasive. The neighbourhood I grew up in, sure, you'd have friends, people you loved, that you'd trust absolutely but never and I truly mean *never* would you demonstrate your feeling in a public fashion.

You ever tried to hug someone there, you'd lose your arm from the elbow. You asked someone,

"How are you?"

It was more likely to mean,

"How are you fixed?"

Meaning do you have money and more importantly, are you willing to give me some?

Ask any Irish woman about her man, about the sweet talk he'd produce, and you'll hear,

"Oh yes, he told me I wasn't the worst."

My parents, I loved them, no question, I never once told them so, as my mother lay dying, fighting for breath, my declaration of love consisted of,

"Can I get you anything?"

I am aware of what a tragedy that is.

So when we came up close and personal with Americans, we were more than a little astounded at their candour.

Tommy, hidden and furtive all his life, both from necessity and nurture, never got a handle on this aspect of America. When we'd worked on the site, we had an apartment in Brooklyn Heights. Flat out, we both loved the area. The apartment was nothing to write home about, two small rooms you could barely swing a cat in.

First night there, we did what you do, if you're Irish, you go the neighbourhood bar. Get orientated. As it goes, we got talking to a guy who worked on the trains. Two beers in, he says,

"I love you guys."

And goes to get us a brew.

Tommy watches him and turns to me, asks,

"What's fucking wrong with him?"

Me, the sophisticated college boy tried,

"He's just been friendly."

Tommy shook his head, said,

"Oh, he's gay."

I kept my voice low, said,

"No, it's the way they are, they're just . . ."

I had to search for a word to capture the essence, attempted,

"Up front."

He actually mouthed the word, let it dance about his mouth, he looked like it didn't fit and he nodded, went,

"So back to my original point, there's something wrong with him."

I told the sad truth, said,

"No, there's something wrong with us."

Sitting on the plane, looking at Bill, his earnest face and the total sincerity with which he'd said he liked me, I felt such a pang of sorrow. And that's the curse of our race, we sure as hell feel the stuff, we just can't express it. Probably why we have so much music.

Bill asked if I'd been to Vegas before and I said no. He assured me I'd have me an experience. The next twenty minutes, we did as they term it, shoot the shit. He told me of other visits to Vegas and various larger-than-life characters he'd met, explained,

"The reason they talk about Vegas rules, what happens in Vegas, stays in Vegas, is not so much discretion as who the hell would believe it?"

I would remember those words and wish I'd paid more attention.

Bill had a wonderful laugh, one of those up from the stomach, the whole system involved, his eyes near distorted from merriment.

I have never laughed like that in my whole life, not even when drink was involved. I did the best I could to join Bill in his hilarity but, as always, I was holding on, that ice control watching every single word. Could almost hear my mother as she'd said and often,

"Stephen, he lives one step away from the rest of us."

Forced myself to relinquish a little of that steel, even told Bill a story about some high jinks in New York. A complete fabrication but to let him see I could be a fun guy.

He bought it.

You were observing us, you'd have seen couple of guys,

letting their hair down, getting in party mode.

Just two guys hitting Vegas, having a high old time. Not twenty-four hours gone, I'd left a man gut shot, leaking blood on a hard floor. Made the big mistake of dozing off.

You wake with a headache and a hard-on. One as painful as the second is useless. We were touching down and the pilot was welcoming us to the Strip, adding,

"Be lucky."

Yeah.

After we disembarked, Bob shook my hand, said,

"Look me up, the Sahara is at the bottom of the Strip, near the Hilton."

I agreed I might and he waddled towards a slot machine, feeding coins into it. I went to collect my bag, noticed the number of men wearing cowboy hats. Tommy would have loved it. There was an air of festivity, adrenaline, and despite my throbbing head, I felt the buzz.

The only piece of Tommy, materially, I possessed was his poems, maybe twenty in all, written in Gothic script in a small leather-bound journal. He said,

"Bruce Chatwin kept his writing in one of those."

The story was Chatwin had them handcrafted in Paris, a story more appealing than truthful. Tommy had handed me the volume on a lads' night out, Siobhan was out on that new ritual, hen night. Translated as "women on the piss."

We were in O'Connor's in Salthill, where you get serious music at a serious juncture in the evening. That holy moment betwixt all out inebriation and simply *feeling mighty*. The band lit the bodhrans, fiddles, then spoons tapping out from the edge of the stage. They were local,

fronted by a feisty girl singer who belted out the songs like
she was raging, spitting iron. No older than twenty but a
voice more ancient than Billie Holiday. I knew her, and off
stage, she was shy, quiet, unremarkable, but hit that stage
and she was Rilke's panther, something primeval un-
leashed. She was doing Neil Young's "Powderfinger," via
The Cowboy Junkies. Tommy reached in his duffel coat,
produced the book, said,

"Some stuff I wrote."

Was astounded, went,

I didn't know you wrote."

He was staring at the girl, tears in his eyes, for Neil
Young, his writing, my comment, shit, could have been the
smoke. The no-smoking edict wasn't due for another
while. He said,

"Man, there's a lot you don't know."

True enough.

I finished my Jameson, tasted good, tasted like...an-
other? I asked,

"Poems?"

He shrugged.

"Poems manqué. I call them tones, lets me off the poetry rap."

Throw a stone in Ireland, you hit a poet, rarely a decent
one. No wonder Tommy wanted out from that category. I
went to open the book and he shouted,

"Jesus, not now, what's the matter with you?"

Good question.

Not one I've ever been able to answer.

In Vegas I opened the book, read the first title:

"A

          Star

               Clandestine."

Un-even-ness
best . . . perhaps
a label is
to how to love
I did
Conduct it poor
Invited all the errors
. . . star insanity
do fate control
I'd near believed
Your star
I've only once
The ever, comprehended

Had just this once, real
Close, this once
Had come

Lost you behind
A star façade
A loss befall
Might write on that
Ill-fated.

I took a deep breath, then noticed the brackets at the bottom of the page and in them were a few more lines, like what? . . . an afterthought, an explanation. Read them aloud to get the taste.

"I only know
the heart exists
on what
it daren't lose."

Put the volume down, only nineteen to go, I'd ration them, have a daily blast of anguish. I didn't try to make sense of them, hell, I'd never made sense of Tommy.

He just was.

No, I'd let it soak, wrap round me for a while, then maybe and big maybe, read it again.

Vegas has towering blocks of hotels, maybe a thousand rooms per hotel and high, fuck, all the way into the skyline. I'd gotten the courtesy coach into the centre and decided to walk the Strip, try to get a sense of the place. The heat was ferocious, within seconds I was drenched, the booze from the flight pouring out of me. I muttered,

"Ah, Tommy. You'd love it here."

Found a two-story hotel and if that wasn't remarkable enough, it was old. Old in America being over fifty years.

La Concha.

Just what I needed . . . a shell. Crouched beneath the shadow of the Riviera and it was cheap. For thirty bucks, I got a huge, old-fashioned room overlooking a garden and pool. A grouchy security guard was patrolling. I said,

"Nice day for it."

He had his hand on the butt of his revolver, gave me the hard stare, asked,

"Why are you staying here?"

He was gnawing at a toothpick, moving it annoyingly from end to end in his mouth. It made a sucking noise, almost wheezing. I went Irish, hit a question with a question. Irritates the shit out of the Brits which is why we do it.

"You don't recommend it?"

More sucking, hitched up his belt, then,

"The ground floor."

"Yeah?"

"Where you got your ice machine, you got your wet-backs."

I wanted to go,

"Give me your poor, your downtrodden."

Not lines that had made much impact on him, I took a guess, said,

"They're in the catering trade."

He spat, thick phlegm over the balcony, hoping to hit a wetback, no doubt, he said,

"They're a pain in the ass is what they is."

I nodded, said,

"Nice talking to you."

Turned the key in my room, an actual key, not the card gig.

How old is that?

The guard added before I closed the door,

"Not much longer."

"Excuse me?"

"This joint, they're gonna knock it."

I reached for levity, tried,

"Not today, I hope?"

"Not goddamn soon enough, you ask me."

I got in the room, unpacked, noticed there was no kettle, just the basics, bed and phone. Thomas Merton style. The army had me familiar with that routine. I'd stopped at a liquor store, bought a bottle of Stoli, poured an Irish measure (generous), took a hefty swig. The thirst I'd always controlled was rearing up, refusing to be denied. I don't know, was it shooting Juan, Tommy's writing, Vegas, but for once, I said the biker's version of the Serenity Prayer: Fuck it.

Was going to see where the booze took me. I should have been phoning Siobhan, I should have been covering my ass. Should, should, should.

Poured another.

"Please don't put your life in the hands of a rock and roll band who'll throw it all away."

— OASIS, "Don't Look Back in Anger"

DADE WAS FEELING the miles. All-night driving, behind a speed jag, will take it out of you, nine ways through Sundays. He jammed to a halt, parked like he didn't give a fuck, which he didn't, muttered,

"Caffeine."

Stomped into the diner, slid into a booth and the waitress, approached, said,

"How you doing, honey?"

He glared at her, spat,

"Coffee, gallon of it, grits and eggs over easy, some toast and don't burn it."

She stared at him but the scar on his face gave her pause, he was wearing shades but she could sense the ferocity and said,

"Be just a mo'."

He popped a speed, crunching it between the wedge of Juicy Fruit and waiting for the jolt. A magazine was on the seat and he spotted an article on Mötley Crüe. Man, he loved those guys, "Girls, Girls, Girls," he'd got down and dirty with that song like, more times.

He read with growing disbelief, Mick Mars had a hip replacement, Vince Neil had $70,000 worth of plastic surgery for a reality show. Nikki had quit drinking and Tommy was sounding like an advertisement for rehab. As his chow arrived, he flung the mag aside, said,

"Pathetic crew, more like."

The speed kicked in as he chewed on the grits but it didn't lighten his mood. When the Crüe blew it, it could happen to anyone. He drank three mugs of coffee and left a dollar for the tip. The waitress couldn't help it, said as he opened the door,

"You come back and see us soon."

He let his shades slide, let her see what he was thinking and she pulled way back, he said,

"Count on it, sweet thing."

Dade rolled into Tucson, the baseball mitt in his lap, a fresh stick of Juicy Fruit in his cheek, rolling it against his gums, making sucking noises as he drew the sweetness deep. The lightning scar was itching and he dabbed at it. He was feeling antsy, his supply of speed getting dangerously low. Plus, the little girl, she'd obviously been pulled out of the SUV. But he should have made sure. He slapped his hand against the wheel, went,

"Fuck it."

The tape was playing

"Let's Play House."

The irony was lost on him. The picture of Tammy seemed to be staring at him, he threw a punch at her, asked,

"The fuck you looking at?"

Then, ground on the accelerator, added,

"Bitch."

Tucson confused him, he'd been driving for fifteen minutes and had yet to find the core. No building was over two stories and it appeared like one lengthy suburb, he shouted,

"Where's the goddamn centre?"

What he wanted was downtown, a central area with Wal-mart, Starbucks, lowlifes, a place he could blend.

Some redneck had told him Tucson was a little bit country, a little bit rock 'n' roll. Yeah, but man, heavy on the enchilada, like being in a clean Mexico. Dade had a connection here, for guns and drugs. His contact, a heavy biker named Fer, had set up the meet, Dade had whined,

"Why Tucson?"

Fer, scratching his shaggy beard, creaking in a uniform of denim and old leather, said,

" 'Cos, it's a hop to the border. Where you think the freight is coming from?"

Dade hadn't thought and could give a fuck. What he thought was, score me a case of AK-47s, sell 'em in Detroit. A soul brother had pledged top dollar, the dope was for maintenance.

Ride on.

Dade, as with most of his business, had met Fer in a bar, in El Paso. Now there was a happening place. Bikers and outlaws, drifters from every state, where Dade felt most at home. He sought out the edge, drew adrenaline there. In *Pain Management*, Andrew Vachss describes Dade exactly, says, "Boy like you, you was born trash."

They'd set up to connect in a dive in Tucson, Dade had gone,

"Why can't we do the deal here, in El Paso?"

Fer was drinking Sam Adams, the Boston brew, sucked remnants from the bottle, said,

"The *federales* are watching me."

Put Dade in mind of Willie and Merle, going *mano a mano* on *Pancho and Lefty*, for days after, he'd abandoned Tammy, was humming

"All the *Federales* say . . ."

And couldn't for the life of him bring up the next line, knew it was something about the cops catching the outlaw without too much effort. 'Course, he went back to Tammy, always did, she was like *family*.

He'd stared at Fer, then reached in his satchel, took out a bundle, half now, half on delivery. The satchel was from San Antonio, Dade had gone to see the Alamo and been hugely disappointed it was so small, what was with that? Was impressed with the plaques on the walls, to the Irish who'd died there, 176 of them . . . who'd have known that, the spud eaters, dying for Texas. The Irish were about to cross his path in the near future and leave repercussions he'd never have imagined.

The satchel belonged to a half-caste hooker, he'd beaten the living crap out of her, took the bag as a souvenir, she'd dissed Tammy, lucky he hadn't killed her.

Fer had a woman with him, a feral creature who soaked tequila like a leech, she never spoke, just cut slices of lime, put salt on the side, and knocked back the Mexican hooch like mother's milk. The deal done, Fer stood, said,

"Gotta piss, man."

As it said in *Pulp Fiction*, this was probably more information than Dade needed. Fer lumbered out, his denim/leather creaking like bad news. Dade took a good look at the woman, she'd a set of knockers that put heat in his groin, she caught the look, asked,

"The fuck you staring at?"

He loved it, feisty was near his favourite thing. On the turn of a nickel, he'd have dogged her, then turned her over, cut her throat. He gave her the smile. She was a biker chick, a Mama, had seen badass up close and personal for longer than she dared remember. Psychos, loser's stone killers, she'd partied with the worst of them. But this guy, this was a different species, he'd cut you and not even take count. He'd smile, ice in his veins, and now he said,

"I was wondering, your old man, Fer...what kinda handle is that?"

She wished Fer would come back, she was feeling something she hadn't felt in a long time, fear, answered,

"Short for Lucifer."

Dade loving it, soaking up every hostile vibe available, said,

"He's the devil, huh?"

Fucking with her, she tried for hard, went,

"You better believe it, buster."

Fer was returning, heavy boots thumping along the floor, his flies undone, urine stains along his left jean leg, like a badge of pride, Dade whispered to her,

"I'm a bit of a demon my own self."

* * *

Physically, Dade had more than a passing resemblance to Christopher Walken, not the gorgeous specimen of *The Deer Hunter* . . . no, more the crazed face of later movies where he seemed to have cornered the market in psychos and whackos. Dade believed he looked like Jimmy Woods, especially the Woods of *The Onion Field* and *Salvador*. One of his favourite fantasies was the movie of his life . . . him portrayed as a Dillinger lovable scamp. He'd put J-Lo in there, not that the bitch could act, but he liked that body, get Oliver Stone to direct 'cos that dude was seriously out there.

Fer had suggested Dade stay at La Quinta in Tucson, Dade had asked,

"Why?"

Fer had sniggered, said,

"It's like citizens-ville, lots of wetbacks working there, you get horny, you put it to the housekeeper, like who she's gonna call?"

Where the fuck was it, he pulled up on an avenue, checked the sign, read,

STONE AVENUE

Tickled him. Got a flash of the biker chick, he'd asked her,

"You like Tammy?"

"Who?"

He couldn't credit her, went,

"Who, an American icon, is fuckin' who, Tammy Wynette is who."

She'd been scared, he knew. Fear was near as vital as speed, cranked him way up, she'd said,

"I don't, like, do country and western, I've got the Hole CD."

Figured. Courtney Love, another space cadet.

He hit on her tone, prissy, a middle-class accent overriding the biker front. He let her remark simmer, dance around in the stratosphere, then said,

"Next time we hook up, I'll play you some Tammy, maybe 'Don't Want to Play House,' get you converted."

Considering, after the business, maybe track them, get his green back, put the bitch in the ground, shove a Tammy tape in her mouth, go,

"Now you're country."

And Fer, it would be a real buzz to put out that dude's lights, cancel his ticket.

Getting out of the vehicle, Dade liked the way his boots crunched on the asphalt, popped a Juicy Fruit, had the Walther in his waistband, watched a Mex with his wife and kids, hailed them,

"Yo, Pedro."

The man turned, asked,

"*Qué?*"

Dade eyes him, giving him the yard treatment, thinking, spic city, the guy wearing cowboy boots, Yankees T, and Wranglers, like he was a goddamn white man, Dade decided to fuck with him a little, asked,

"What's with the T, Speedy, like you'd know shit from shinola?"

The wife's eyes widened and before the man could go macho, Dade added,

"*Dónde esta La Quinta?*"

The man conferred with his wife, the kids staring at

Dade, he winked at them, made a gun of his index finger and thumb, dropped the hammer.

The man replied in a burst of Mex, Dade held up a hand, smiled, said,

"Whoa, easy, Miguel, that's about all my spic rap, gotta like ration it, hit me again in *Ingles, comprende, hombre?*"

The man's eyes glowed and Dade felt his adrenaline zoom up a notch, thinking the fuck's got a knife in his boot. Dade could see it, the Walther up and spitting, take 'em down on Stone Avenue, waste the brats first. The man was saying,

"Ees not far, you make a right then along Beaumont, ees past the university, beside Denny's."

He pronounced it Dinny's. Dade figured he'd grab a bowl of chili there, wash it down with some Lone Star, he said,

"Much obliged, pilgrim, I ever need like a gardener or someone to clean my pool, I'll keep you in mind, and hey, great boots."

He burned rubber outa there, got a jump from them. Five minutes later, he was checking into La Quinta, not flash but clean and white, he booked for five nights, asked,

"You got cable?"

"*Sí.*"

Grabbed his key, got squared away. Two beds in the room, coffeemaker, wide-screen TV. He got the coffee going, hit the remote. MTV. The Black Eyed Peas with "Shut Up," he cranked some speed, sang with the hook,

"Shuddup."

Sang loud.

Dade's first serious stretch was when he was twenty, he'd

burgled a house, could have been away clean but spotted a bottle of tequila. Never having tried it, he knew there was some shit involving salt and lime but opted for putting the bottle on his head.

Chug

Chug

That's all she wrote.

Blew him across the room.

He's slumped against a wall, vomit on his front, the empty bottle between his legs when the cops came. This was in Oklahoma, not the best place to be a burglar, especially an inept one. They take property seriously. Too, he was out of state and he was most definitely out of luck. When he opened his eyes, a state trooper named Jones was standing over him, said in a friendly way,

"Tossed your cookies, huh."

Dade was naïve enough to buy the tone. Jones put out his hand, said,

"Lemme give you a hand there, son."

Put out his hand.

Later, when they finally extracted the nightstick from Dade's ass, Jones said,

"Hey, I was looking for that."

The judge, with an equally friendly, warm voice, asked,

"First offence, eh, partner?"

Dade had done a week of lockup, the nightly visits from the deputies, and he was no longer buying warmth. He glared at the judge, who continued,

"Don't see why we should ruin a young life over a youthful prank, you listening to me, son?"

And Dade had dared to breathe.

Got a five-year jolt.

Served every day, came out with a brown paper bag, prison tats, a passion for Tammy Wynette, and a simmering ferocity he'd learned to put behind a smile. Dade had great teeth.

State issue.

First week of the term, a black guy had knocked out his teeth, going,

"Don't need 'em for blow jobs."

Six months later, Dade, a leading light in a white supremacist gang, had taken the guy's eyes out with a spoon. No one fucked with him again.

He'd gotten a queen for his cell, a sissy out of North Carolina, and the bitch had been heavily into Tammy, played her all day. When Dade traded the cow for a piece, he'd kept the Tammy albums.

Speedway Avenue was where the students boogied. Dade, dressed in black 501s, a black T with a red lightning zag, felt it accessorised his scar, reading,

"Metallica."

Figured the students'd dig it. He let the T hang over his jeans, not as a fashion statement but to cover the Walther. No way he was rocking without weight. Last item, the boots, he studied the heels, stacked, getting worn, needed refit, said,

"Fuck it."

Pulled them on, studied himself in the mirror, he'd a toke earlier, chill him out. Liked what he saw, a dude in black, easy smile and crinkly lines round the eyes. Pass for Clint Eastwood's son. Maybe he'd score a college chick, give her a touch of the hard country. The baseball mitt was on the bed, he picked it up, smelled the old leather, made him sigh. Been a shame to waste the kid, he'd an arm on him and catch, shit, that kid had eyes in the back of his skull. Then he giggled, feeling the gun buck in his hand, giving Ben, the kid, a third eye. He put the mitt in his satchel, the maids, wetbacks, they'd steal anything. He raised his palm to his reflection, asked,

"Give me five, bro?"

He slapped his hand against the glass, then made a clicking sound with his tongue, said,

"Let's boogie."

The glass guy winked.

> "Sherry was juicily conceived, but Marie squeezed
> even more out of her, flirting coyly with Sterling
> Hayden, conniving with Vince Edwards, snidely
> blowing smoke up Elisha Cook's aspirations."
>
> — EDDIE MULLER,
> *Dark City: The Lost World of Film Noir*

THE FIRST BAR, Dade lucked out, scored a few tabs of E from a student who said,

"Like the shirt."

He was cruising, on his third bar he switched from long necks to Wild Turkey, tried a line on some girls but they blew him off. He shrugged, the night was young.

Moved on to Fourth Avenue, the bars had live music, he pushed through the crowd, asked the lead singer of a country band.

"You do Tammy Wynette?"

The guy was sweating, his cowboy shirt soaked, and he stared at Dade, said,

"Get fucking real, pal."

Dade's mood switched, he went to the barren area of his soul without a change of expression, nodded, moved away. The guy, emboldened, shouted,

"Wynette is so, like, yesterday."

The use of her surname inflamed Dade's building storm, he took up a position against the wall, drink in his fist, murder in his heart. The place was hopping, people having themselves a time. The singer launched into a Garth Brooks song:

"Friends in Low Places."

Dade fucking loathed Brooks, wondered what next? Thinking, Vince Gill?

Sure enough.

Some dirge about a gold ring. Dade drained his glass, felt the Turkey hit his gut like acid, he hailed a passing waitress, dressed in cowgirl mode, asked,

"Yo, hon, get me a tequila sunrise."

She glared at him, snapped,

"I'm not your hon."

His barometer hit top, Def Con 1, he'd have backhanded the bitch but he'd registered the bouncers.

Apes.

Not to be fucked with. Across the room, he felt eyes on him, his paranoia, always cooking, was at max. A blond woman but older than most of the patrons, staring at him. He was distracted by the return of the waitress, who pushed the drink at him, he asked,

"You'll be wanting a tip?"

Her freeze thawed a bit and she nearly smiled. He added,

"Watch your mouth."

Gulped the drink, then looked across the room, no sign of the blonde. Shit. So back to monitoring the singer. Three numbers, the guy was chugging Buds, he had to piss, right? Two Reba McEntire numbers later, the guy hopped off the stage, headed for the restroom, Dade moved. The head was outside, across a car park, Dade hung back, let the other cowboys exit then followed. The singer was zipping up, whistling. Was it Elvis's "American Trilogy?"

Dade crushed his skull with the butt of the Walther, pulled him into a booth, rifled his jeans, a roll of twenties, two joints and a tab of acid. Dade popped it, then smashed the guy's nose, muttering,

"Nobody, and I mean fucking no one, disses Tammy."

He got outside, took a deep breath, saw the blonde woman at the door of the club, staring at him, a half smile playing the corners of her mouth, then she went back inside, he muttered,

"The fuck's going on?"

And went after her. Found her at the bar, asked,

"I know you?"

She was ordering tequila shots, had the salt and lime at the ready, she asked,

"We won't be seeing Garth Brooks for a while, am I right?"

The smile on her mouth, so he asked,

"You like Tammy Wynette?"

The woman laughed, said,

"The beat of my heart."

Then sang the opening line to "Honey (I Miss You)."Slid a shot glass towards him, he asked,

"You wanna chow down?"

A raised eyebrow, then,

"What had you in mind?"

He went for it, said,

"Navy beans with ham over corn bread, collard greens, stewed turnips on the side, redneck cuisine."

He leaned on the *cuisine*. Make-or-break-time.

She downed the shot, asked,

"The hell we waiting for?"

Linked his arm going out, he curtsied to the bouncers, said,

"Y'all have a good one."

They gave him the steel face. He asked her,

"So hon, you got a name?"

She was right in beside him, her perfume doing jigs on his head, said,

"Sherry."

A large bankroll consisting mainly of singles with a
hundred on the outside is called a "Michigan Roll."

— TOM KAKONIS, *Michigan Roll*

A SPORTING SPECTACLE of real violence was spreading
through America. Named "Toughman," it was started by a
Michigan millionaire fight promoter. Ordinary men and
women, with no training, no experience, pull on gloves,
headgear, climb into a ring and go for it. The prizes are not
the lure, never amounts to more than fifty bucks, this
keeps it at amateur level and thus free from government
monitoring.

People flock to the events, at more than 130 impromptu
venues across the land. Over 500,000 paid to watch last
year. Four people had been killed in that period, adds to the
attraction, come see some poor schmuck get his or hers, in-
cite the fighters to extreme behaviour. A contestant, before
entering the ring, signs a waiver, acknowledging the possibility of serious injury or death.

Possibility.

Paramedics are on hand but no doctors, are you kidding?

The referees are not required to prove experience in the craft.

Dade spent three days holed up with Sherry. Booze, sex, dope, and Tammy. He never even got a chance to be vaguely homicidal. She'd a villa near a motel called the Lazy 8. He asked,

"How come you live in a house, there's a dude ranch in like, spitting distance?"

She'd given him a look, part amusement, part irked, said,

"A girl needs privacy."

Which he thought was rich, she hadn't worn a stitch for three days. Now she was pulling on track gear and he asked,

"You jog?"

Answered out of the corner of her mouth, a cig going on the other end, said,

"Yeah, right."

Then added,

"I look like I'm from where, stupid town?"

He was getting dangerously low on speed, the ants gnawing at his nerve ends, his teeth grinding, his left eye giving an involuntarily twitch, she asked,

"You like to fight?"

She kept doing that, coming at him from left field. He was up, pacing, said,

"I've had a few,"

Yeah, like duh.

And he near sang,

"But then again, too few too."

She ordered,

"Get your ride, we're going to a rumble."

Gave him directions to an area outside the city limits. He'd Tammy on the speakers, with "Please Come to Boston". When he saw the line of cars, pickups, Harleys, he thought it was a concert but said nothing. Parked next to a couple of hogs, glanced at her, a wild excitement in her eyes. Hundreds of people, electricity in the air. Grabbing his hand, she pulled him through and he saw a makeshift ring, two guys walloping the crap out of each other, he said,

"Boxing."

A touch of spittle on her lip, she gasped,

"Way more than that."

The bout ended when one of the guys went down. The ring was cleared and the referee shouted,

"Next up is Kate the Kat, all the way from Noo Orleans."

A black girl, early twenties, in shorts, T, and sneakers, hopped into the ring. She was fit, athletic, looked like she worked out. A lot. Sherry asked,

"Like that?"

"She's fit."

Sherry sniggered, said,

"I'm so going to whup her black ass."

Before he could squeal,

"What?"

The referee asked who was willing to step to the plate, get themselves fifty bucks, Sherry's hand was waving and to the cheers of the crowd, she climbed into the ring. Dade shook his head, she was an itsy bitsy thing, sure she had spunk but the nigger would chew her ass. Sherry was pulling the gloves on and to the roars of the crowd, refused the protective helmet. The referee blew a whistle and they went at it. Any other time, Dade would have got off on chicks mixing it. But this was a Tammy acolyte, not too many no more. The ones who'd held the torch longest were beginning to desert to Dolly Parton.

How sad was that?

Sherry was taking a beating. Once, twice, the black girl caught her smack in the kisser. A hillbilly beside Dade, nudged him in the ribs, said,

"Yer gal, she's getting thrashed."

You poked Dade in the ribs, you better be carrying, but he was too distracted. A guy was making book at the side, all the green going on the black chick, Dade put a twenty on her his own self, might as well get something for the trip.

Ouch, Sherry took a sucker to the gut, staggered, the crowd chanted,

"Give it up, girl."

Dade didn't think she'd last the round. The black was grinning, easiest fifty she'd ever earn plus she got to kick white ass. The bell went, Sherry retreated to her corner, Dade fought his way through, said,

"Babe, give it up, she's killing you."

And Sherry smiled, blood pouring from her mouth, gasped,

"You think so, huh?"

Then added,

"Put two large on me, to win."

He did, reluctantly, and the bookie gave him a look of pity.

THE BLACK GIRL did a little dance, then a tap routine in the centre of the ring, the crowd loving it. Sherry looked at Dade, said,

"Bring it on, bitch."

Made her way into the centre, swaying slightly, as if she was about to drop, the black girl put her hands on her lips, sneered,

"Forgot your lip gloss, mama?"

And was lifted clear off her feet by a left hook from Sherry, the clean crunch of her jaw breaking, a collective gasp from the crowd, especially Dade.

That's all she wrote.

Flat on her back, a moan trying to form. Sherry stood over her, planted a dainty foot on her belly, looked up, said,

"White power."

The crowd erupted, wild screaming, roars of approval,

the referee pulled Sherry off, her mouth streaming blood, counted out the black, Sherry demanded,

"Where's my fifty bucks?"

Coming out of the ring, the hillbilly passed her a bottle of shine, she put it on its head, drank deep, then shouted,

"Nigrah in her place."

More acclaim, she took another swig then hurled the shine over the crowd, blessing them in hooch and bigotry. Dade collected his winnings, the bookie, stunned, went,

"What a pistol."

Dade, grin ear to ear, pulled her into his vehicle. Could feel the adrenaline burning off her, she said,

"Let's fuck."

They did.

Then to Denny's, ordered steaks and grits, he'd brought along a batch of Coors. Sherry still in her bloodied gear, the waitress staring wide eyed. Dade raised his bottle, said,

"You had me going there."

His prick still ached from the sex, Sherry stabbed at her split lip, said,

"I had help."

"What?"

She opened her right hand, a chunk of lead in there. Dade whistled, acknowledged,

"Babe, you've got you some moves."

Later, in the villa, downing shots of bourbon, Sherry, her mouth coming off his dick, asked,

"Think you could waste a dude for me?"

He shrugged, asked,

"What he'd do?"

"Gut shot my old man."

Dade drained his glass, asked,

"You miss him, huh, your old man?"

Her mouth turned down, she spat,

"He was a cocksucker."

Then she hit the shower, singing, if he wasn't mistaken,

"Blanket on the Ground."

If he wasn't hitting a speed burn he'd have joined her, his body was going into tremens, she came out, buck naked, looked at him, asked,

"You hurtin', baby?"

"What?"

"Got yourself a dose of the crank blues, a little short maybe?"

Yet again she was out of left field, he decided to fess up, said,

"Yeah, some, my um, meds are a little low, not like I'm some kind of lame addict bu you know."

Sherry had pulled on a black halter top, not as tight as skin but akin to strangulation, then sat on the bed to pull on tight white jeans, finally she stood, cocked a hip, asked,

"What you need, fellah? I got, uppers, downers, side-winders, ludes, crystal, jitter bugs, black beauties, white juice . . ."

And stopped.

He didn't know if she was yanking his chain, had never heard of some of these, asked,

"You yanking my chain?

She checked her boobs in the mirror, juggled around to get them up and frisky, said,

"I never kid about dope."

He had to know, asked,

"Where'd you get them?"

And she turned, her eyes with a cold slant, said,

"My old man was in the business, let's say I took some samples."

He was delighted, went,

"Bring it on."

She did.

A black vanity case, opened it, his jaw dropped. In alphabetical order, neatly arranged, more dope than in a Hunter S. Thompson trip. She went to S, pulled out some cellophane, dumped a rash of pills on the bed. He was mesmerised, said,

"Let's start at A."

She shut the case, put a finger to her lips, said,

"Sh . . . sh, God doesn't like greedy boys."

He dry popped a pill, crushed it with his prison molars, tasted the acrid bent, asked,

"Like you believe in God?"

Kidding, gently fucking with her, lust in his blood, he could play around and she gave the answer that bought his soul, said,

"He gave us Tammy Wynette, what's not to believe?"

He gave the only answer available:

"Amen, sister."

On the Sonoran Desert in Arizona, sixteen Titan II
missiles bearing nuclear warheads stood through
the Cold War in a circle of power around the city of
Tucson.

— DENIS JOHNSON, *Seek: Reports from the Edges of
America and Beyond*

A DAY LATER, Dade went to La Quinta, checked out, he'd
tops . . . spent half an hour there. The manager looked at
the dollar bills and Dade went,

"Got a problem, buddy?"

Let just a little edge slide into his tone.

The man, from Baja, sighed, said,

"We, how you say, anticipate credit card?"

Dade liked the dude, the way his hands shook as he
handled the crumpled bills, with obvious distaste, Dade
went on the offensive, not feeling it but just for practice,
growled,

"What, you have a lot of American Express in Wetback-
ville or where ever the fuck you crawled out of, huh, that
it, you implying there's something with my cash money,
with the currency of these here UNITED STATES . . .?"

Roared the latter, spittle flying out to land on the guy's
collar, the guy eyeing it but hadn't the balls to wipe it, he'd

given one brief look into Dade's eyes and that was plenty, said,

"No, ees fine. I get you receipt."

Dade fired up a Lucky, his usual Kools had run out, no smoking decals were all over the lobby, Dade said,

"What you can get me, *amigo*, is a reduction. I never even slept in the goddamn room."

The manager split the bundle in two, moved one wedge to Dade. Picking up the cash, Dade said,

"You could pass for white, fellah, I tell you, bro, I run into you at any of the watering holes, I'll let you buy me a brewski, how does that work for you, that grease your wheels?"

The manager thought if he ever saw Dade again, he'd head for the hills. He said,

"*Buena suerte.*"

"Yeah, like, whatever."

Back at the villa, he heard Tammy with "Apartment Number Nine" . . . he loved that tune. He was feeling something totally alien, he was feeling admiration, for Sherry. It was not a concept he had much trade with, his norm, if such a term could be applied to a stone killer, was gratification and aggression. What he wanted, he wanted now and if heads got bent in the process, then all the better.

Sherry brought him to a low dive, the kind of place that catered to the outcast, spit on the floor, blood on the counter, a happening joint.

Plus, it had a jukebox, oh Lordy, cranking out, Hank Williams, AC/DC, Kid Rock, White Stripes, Vegas, and yes, Herself, Tammy.

What they call . . . an eclectic mix.

Sherry was explaining to him the formula for Long Island Tea, that type of rap, where logic never darkened the flow, he listened then sneered,

"Fucking yuppie shit."

She was looking across the bar, a bunch of renegades mixing it with some Mexicans, you could tell one of the parties was on Crystal, the body language shouted *blood*. She turned to Dade, asked,

"You ever hook up before?"

For the thousandth time, he'd reply as he near always did to her with the tiresome,

"What?"

Like some broken down parrot who'd squawk the one word and squander it mercilessly. She was on Easy Times, the bottle on the table, that kind of place and it was sliding down smooth, she said,

"You ever buddy up, like, have a partner?"

He felt he was a level up, a bottle of Makers near his Zippo, nice as a Democrat and he laughed,

"What, I've got one now?"

The *what* word still in currency.

She let it cruise, waited.

Dade had never shared, never was long enough with anyone to tell them details. But Sherry had him turned inside out and to his amazement, he began,

"Time ago, a woman, Karen with two kids, separated from Glen, her old man, I was with her for like..."

Jeez, how long, he couldn't recall. The woman had been hurting and he slid in there, Mr. Nice Guy, all laid-back concern, no push, chilled, and she'd bought it. Hadn't moved into her home but real close. Took Ben, the kid, for ball practice, came to really connect with the boy, started to believe it was his kid, the battered mitt, he imagined it had been in the family for generations. The girl, though, now okay, some problems there. She never took to him. He'd given her a CD of Tammy and the cunt went,

"She's like, old."

Let that go, treated the mom like fucking royalty. He'd been having the time of his life, buying fully into the whole scenario. One day, in the park, the picnic, the whole nine, gingham table cloth, Tupperware, fried chicken, apple pie (home baked).

A woman passing going,

"Nice to see a family."

Then to hell and gone.

Ol' Glen came back, the prick. Got himself on some goddamn 12 Step program and Dade . . . Dade was like yesterday. So he'd hung around, hung around a lot, made some, okay, threats.

He was kiddin', c'mon, as if he'd hurt his own kin? What they do?

Took off is what.

Upped and ran. In the old SUV.

Dade had come ambling towards their front door, nice and mellow, no biggie. The Walther held real loose in his right hand and so okay, maybe he'd let off a round, nothing major, not like he had a MAC machine gun in his arms and was spraying willy-nilly like some pissed-off postal stiff.

He was just, what do you call it, getting their attention, I mean goddamn it, they weren't taking his calls, so like, what's a guy to do?

Write them a letter.

Yeah, right, that would work.

Wiped his brow.

And what they do, were they willing to come out or better yet, invite him in, have a few brews, maybe not Glen, a soda for that alky, and talk the misunderstanding over. Thrash it out as his dad used to say and he giggled, remembering how his ol' dad thrashed as he put him under the water for the last time.

No, the mad bastards, they jumped in the vehicle and took off. No *see you soon buddy* or *water the lawn for us.* Nope, just upped and lit out. He roared after them,

"NOTHING WORKS ON IT, THE BELT'S FRAYED, THE LOCK'S FUCKED."

And well, he guessed they didn't hear him. But hey, guess what?

He caught them.

Sweat was pouring down his body, getting in his eyes, Sherry squeezed his leg, said,

"Okay baby, it's okay, they fucked you good."

And he near upturned the table, snarled,

"No, I fucked them good."

Too loud.

The roughnecks looked over, she continued to massage him and he reined it in. She moved, wiped blood from his mouth, he'd near bitten through his tongue, she got another splash of drinks, and he pulled way back. She studied him, said,

"You remind me of someone, an actor?"

He waited, waited for Jimmy Woods and got,

"Chris Walken, I saw him in Bloomingdale's one time, buying socks."

He let it go, enough heat for one occasion. After midnight they got out of there, could hear Willie on the jukebox.

"There were seven Spanish angels."

Dade was having a high old time, laughing, giggling . . . a good old boy, whooping it up, his gal in tow, said,

"Hon, I gotta take a piss."

An alleyway beside the bar, he stumbled into it, singing with the outlaw, a shit-eating grin on his face, trying to find his fly, bursting fit to blow, got his zip down, his hand against the wall and as he let loose, sighed,

"Ah . . ."

Few things to equal that relief and got a blow to his shoulder.

Hurt.

His collar grabbed, pulled round and a broken bottle against his neck, a wild-eyed cowboy, long hair to his shoulders, denim jacket, going,

"Gimme your money, motherfucker."

Late twenties, a scar on his left cheek, a stench of garlic, booze on his breath, Dade whined,

"Don't hurt me, mistah."

Got a nice whimper in there, the guy getting off on it, going,

"I'll cut you, fucker, open you like a bitch, see if I don't."

Dade let his voice rise,

"Please, mistah, I got maybe four hundred bucks in my jeans, take it all, and welcome, lemme get it for you."

And the dumb fuck moved back. Dade had to work at not smiling, the guy went,

"And you can blow me, you'd like that bitch, huh, you do me good, maybe I won't cut you."

Began to reach to his groin, Dade had a flash of the joint, when they knocked his teeth out, saw a white shimmer before his eyes, then his knee came up, the guy doubled over, going,

"Aw, man."

Sherry was there, her face lit, asking,

"He was going to rob you?"

Like she couldn't believe it, she picked up the broken bottle, her face flush with excitement, said,

"Think he's got some balls on him, think I should take them off him?"

Dade thought so.

She did.

Took a time.

IT WAS NIGH IMPOSSIBLE to spook Dade, he was the one who spooked people. Sleeping with Sherry came as near as he was ever going to get. He noticed her fumble under the pillow one night after they'd had wild sex, grabbed her hand, asked, playful,

"Whatcha hiding there, babe?"

And got the demented look, he'd seen it before on the lifers in lockup, the guys who were never getting out, it's not a hopelessness, it's an expression of knowing they're going to hell and just calculating how many they're taking along. He'd figured she'd stashed a little pick-me-up, some ludes, maybe, to keep the heebie-jeebies at bay, he certainly understood that gig. But this feral face, he was stunned, said,

"Whoa, lighten up, babe, I'm not gonna take anything away from you."

The walking dead in the joint, you saw them at chow

time, the way they protected a dish of rice pudding like it was the most precious item on earth. In the scheme of things there, it was close to that. She turned for a second and then a knife was at his throat, not just any old blade but a lethal double-edged piece of mayhem. Worse, it had the sheen of being well used. She snarled, in a tone like a rabid coyote,

"Don't you ever grab my hand, I'll slit you like a snake before you blink."

Her eyes were virtual slits, and a dribble of spittle leaked from the corner of her mouth, the blade was still pushed into his throat so he said in his real mellow voice,

"Sure, babe, whatever you say."

He wanted to go,

"Take a fucking chill pill."

Her hand shook and he wondered if he'd have time to move, then suddenly a spasm hit her, and she dropped the knife, fell back to sleep. He waited a few minutes to make sure she was really out, even lifted the lid of her right eye, the eyeball had rolled all the way back, like a corpse. He eased out of bed, got his Walther, racked the slide but gently, and for a brief moment, considered putting two in her demented skull.

Then his own particular brand of lunacy kicked in and he laughed out loud, said,

"What a rush."

He poured a large shot of Wild Turkey, did a little meth, raised his glass, toasted her with,

"You crazy broad."

From then on, after they made love or whatever you'd

term a form of near mortal combat with sex, he'd slip out of bed, sleep on the floor. No sense in taking chances.

The morning after the knife incident, she woke and was her own sweet self, as if she had no memory of the event, she asked,

"You sleep good?"

Something like real affection in her voice, as if she actually cared, he said,

"Like a baby."

And got a smile that was as close to sanity as he'd ever witness.

He kept the Walther under his own pillow from then on.

I GOT MARRIED.

Oh.

And

lost Tommy's book of writing.

That's where the booze took me.

Britney Spears preceeded me down the aisle a year before in the same church and it would last about the same length of time. She of course went global with the news, my impact was less resounding though equally stupid.

How it went.

Standing in my room at La Concha, I'd taken that long pull of vodka and consciously decided to ride the wind. Perhaps Tommy's death, the bank heist, departing Ireland, betraying Siobhan with Sherry, gut shooting Juan, perhaps they were the cause or . . . I simply figured *enough already* . . . go for it.

Did I ever.

You take an anal-retentive, big on control, remove the brakes and stand way back, it ain't going to be pretty.

It wasn't.

Fuelled on that one drink, I hit the Strip like a banshee, wailing and wild. Circus Circus was advertising margaritas at a buck a throw, sounded good.

I sunk a line of them, those suckers, they slide on easy, each one whispering *more.* I answered the call. Played some blackjack and you need to focus, lost a bundle. The only game I really know, have played with intent, is poker. The Sands had a game going nonstop but I decided to leave it till I got straight, splurged money on roulette, shots, waitresses.

The Peppermill Diner, open 24/7, had waitresses with legs that don't quit. Ever. You go in early morning, bleary eyed, guys with cowboy hats everywhere, and the waitress, before you say a word, asks,

"Bloody Mary?"

Christ, yes.

I thought it was just me. Looked round, the cowboys all got one, came with a mess of reen sticking out, like a mini Vietnam, the waitress named Donna, went,

"Lose the vegetation, right?"

I nodded, my head on fire.

Brought it back, sans garden, goes,

"Fix you right up."

The future Mrs. Blake.

Got the drink down and miracle, felt healed, had me a full breakfast. A few more mornings, Donna and me were old friends. She had a face like a young Mary Tyler Moore,

I'm a sucker for that, the mix of pain and vulnerability. Clearing away the debris of my breakfast, she said,

"I finish at noon."

I didn't know what day it was, had it been a week, a month in Las Vegas, worse, I didn't care. I asked,

"Wanna hang out?"

Like what . . . at the mall?

Jesus, talk about lame.

She gave me a radiant smile, said,

"I love your accent."

The booze said,

"I love you."

I'd forgotten my resolve to work on my accent, had forgotten a whole heap of things, call Siobhan, the moment of shooting Juan, bedding Sherry, but no, not Tommy, his spirit was in every drink, every glass raised, I could see his smile.

1:30, I met her at the Venetian. She'd changed into a tight black top, faded jeans, Reeboks. Looked like gorgeous. We had a meal, as if we were in Italy, the whole of that country reproduced in the Venetian, even gondolas on a canal, I'm praying we didn't go on one. What I most recall is she was from Dayton, Ohio, and she liked to gamble, well, she was with me, perhaps the biggest gamble. I was having the time of my life and in some casino, asked,

"Want to get married?"

Next thing, we're in a limo, going for a licence, down the bad side of town. Gangbangers on the pavement, giving the dead eye. I was drunk enough to seem sober, you don't get a licence if you *display evidnce of intoxication*.

Next day, we're at the Little White Chapel and Elvis is

marrying us. He looked more like George Bush but at least had the moves.

I woke up the next morning, hangover kicked in.

Mercilessly.

I looked round at an opulent room, clothes scattered everywhere, champagne bottles lined up along the wall.

Empty.

I crawled out of bed, got a peek at the hotel stationery ... Excalibur ... serious bucks. Heard a groan, saw I hadn't been alone in the bed. My finger itched and I saw a gold band. Stared back at the bed.

My wife.

A song uncoiling in my head, like a snake of dementia. "Methamphetamine Blues," by Mark Lanegan Band, gritty and noir.

Later, in Tucson, when so much blood had flowed, at reception in the Lazy 8, I'd be given a package. Opened it to find a CD by Patty Griffin and a note saying

Because

I

Loved

You

Donna

Yeah.

Noir that.

That afternoon, in Tucson I'd a few Sam Adams, no vodka, not no more, I waited till I'd sank the third beer, played Patty Griffin.

Fuck.

Killer.

A track, highlit in gold, went to that first, the beers rid-

ing point, I could take it, almost, titled, "Nobody's Cryin'."
A line there, about when you wake in the morning, may
the voice of anxiety become the voice of angels . . . fast-
forwarded to a Bruce song, "Stolen Car," figured that was
safe.

Figured wrong.

Opening line . . . we got married and drifted apart. Ripped
off the headphones, got out of there. In the motel corridor, I
realised I was carrying the CD, let it drop to the floor, the
carpet ensured it didn't make as much as a murmur.

But Vegas, staring at Donna, her asleep, I near shouted,
"The fuck I've done?"

Stumbled through the day, Donna all lit up, and come
evening, safe-ish side of some margaritas, I said,
"I want a divorce."

Her face crumbling, I launched into a drunken rap about
what a class act she was, great lady but she didn't need to
be hitched to a ne'er-do-well, I actually used that term, a
measure of my panic.

As I fumbled on, tripping over the clichés, spilling medi-
ocrity upon garbage, she toyed with the shiny new band on
her wedding finger, interrupted me with,

"You told me about Tucson, about some dude ranch
with the name . . . Lazy 8?"

I held my breath, Jesus, did I mention Siobhan, she said,
"I want to go to Ireland."

"What?"

Her ring was off now, sitting in the middle of the table,
like recrimination with a dull sheen; she added,

"You can have the divorce but I want a trip to Ireland."

My face betrayed me as she said,

"On my own, I guess."

Took two days and a shitpile of cash to get the marriage . . . gone. A lawyer, smooth talker, offered my *drinking problem* as grounds. I was continually half in the bag, so it wasn't difficult to pass. The deal done, Donna and I were standing outside the Bellagio, my eye further down the Strip, past the store that sold Western gear to a sign flicking *Liquor*. I handed her a fat envelope, said,

"You'll love Ireland."

She stared at me, then reached out her hand, I flinched, anticipating a slap. No, she touched my face with her fingers, said,

"I'd have been real good to you."

I had no answer. She turned, walked towards the Riviera, I waited a few rapid beats of my heart, then headed for the off-licence. A priest or chaplain was standing in the midday heat, had a box, asking for donations for the homeless, I dropped my wedding ring in there.

Another week to pull out of the spiral, lie in bed for two days, puking, sweating, hallucinating, swallowing aspirin. The room was like a slaughterhouse. Fourth day, I sipped a Bud Light which is as hellish as it gets, and began the crawl back. My psyche had taken a ferocious beating and I tried to get some food in. Rationed a six of the Light over some more confused days till, finally, food was staying put and the snakes were hissing less in my head. Got out on the Strip, legs shaky and into the shopping mall, to Macy's, bought a mess of new gear but couldn't buy off the recent past.

By the Friday, my hands had stopped shaking and I could

almost function, I attempted an accounting of my financial situation. Had blown a blitzkrieg in my credit. I dreaded to think what Siobhan would make of it, kept postponing the call, knew she'd hear the actual tremor in my voice.

No more gambling or vodka. I went to the movies, saw the wondrous *Lost in Translation*, walked the Strip a thousand times, get my energy back.

Restore, restore, restore.

The commando exercises I'd learned in the army were notable for their gruelling, harsh requirements, went at those like a demon. The sheer punishment helped the guilt, not a whole lot but when you're hurting physically, the mental stuff moves back a notch. By Tuesday, I was able to relish a shower.

An afternoon, walking the Strip, getting my wind back, the heat was beating down, felt it was a good way to sweat out them toxins, and man, did I have a whole truck of those babies.

I decided on a pit stop at the Mirage, keeping my eyes averted from the simulated volcano, I'd had all the explosions I could handle.

Watched the craps table for a bit, they say it's the glamour point of the gaming floor, but then, they say all kinds of shit in Vegas. There seemed to be lot of hollering and shouting, I headed for the bar, asked for a large Coke, laced with ice. A guy on the stool next to me, extended his hand, said,

"Reed, from out of Long Island."

Looked like a hardass, trucker's hands but had a warmth. I shook and he said,

"What about the Sox?"

He laughed at my blank look, went,

"You're Irish, huh?"

He told me the Boston Red Sox, back in 1920, had sold the legendary Babe Ruth, *the bambino.*

Prior to that, the Sox had won five World Series. After the Babe left, they won no more for the rest of the century. He waited for my response, I said,

"Bummer."

I was afraid to ask if we were talking about baseball, I was Irish but did I want to appear totally pig ignorant?

No.

He sighed, continued, the team always lost in game seven. Now he was talking my language, superstition, omens, jinx, curse, we wrote the book on that gig. He took a deep breath, said,

"Then the mothers, they stage the greatest comeback in history by beating the Yankees and taking the title."

A silence followed and finally I said,

"Nice one, eh."

He was disgusted, near spat,

"I'm a New Yorker, do the goddamn math."

What I did was, I got the hell out of there.

The next evening, feeling stronger, dressed in fresh white shirt, new Calvin jeans, mocs, headed for the Sahara. Checked out the celebrity poker, word was that Ben Affleck, David Schwimmer were in attendance.

Nursing an iced coffee, heard,

"Yo . . . buddy?"

Turned, to see the fat man, couldn't get his name, from the plane, dressed in a Western shirt, pearl buttons, and I hope not, but alas, Bermuda shorts, real bad idea. Despite the freezing air conditioning, he had a line of perspiration on his brow, he extended a huge hand, said,

"Bob Milovitz."

And I added,

"Outta Chicago."

He lit up, said,

"You remember, but am I surprised? . . . As those British say . . . not a jot."

He did a passable accent, like a guy who'd watched a lot of *Masterpiece Theatre*, then he went,

"But not an accent you're wanting to hear, am I right? Don't tell me . . . lemme see if I got it . . . Steve . . . yeah, that's it."

I nodded and he stared at my coffee, asked,

"That . . . like . . . a coffee . . . in Vegas, in a casino?"

I put it on the tray of a cruising waitress, she was a looker and legs . . . oh, god. Bob asked,

"Wanna grab a beer, bring me up to speed?"

I remembered I liked him from the off, he had that innate decency. The thinking goes, *Fat people are jolly* and there's an inclination in there, like, *They fucking better be* and it's a crock. Some of the meanest fuckers to come down the pike were carrying weight in every sense.

Really wanted to ask,

"The Sox, baseball right?"

But went the safety route, remarked he was still here?

I didn't ask him how long that was, lest he tell me. I'd paid my bill at La Concha a few days back, and managed to block out the actual length of time of my stay; the receptionist said,

"You must like it here."

That was confirmation enough and the security guard now went,

"Yo, Steve."

Anytime I had the misfortune to run into him.

One evening he'd sneered,

"Got a load on there, pal."

Being a juice head himself, I'd obviously risen in his estimation. Bob said,

"I've been back and forth, maybe three times since we met."

Shit.

He continued,

"The cards, Steve, I do love to play poker, last night, with a pair of Kings, I cleaned out a couple of good ol' Texas boys. What'd you say, we grab a couple of cold ones? The bar guy here, he was in the service, like you."

I noted he'd remembered that, said,

"Sure."

Propped at the bar, we were welcomed warmly by the tender, got some long necks, clinked bottles, Bill going,

"Gimme the good word."

The best I had was Irish, so,

"Slainte."

You say it like you were German with a lisp; he answered,

"Back at you."

He near drained his in one, ordered more. The beer was good, cold, refreshing, beads of moisture creasing the label, the sound of the casino as point, I let my muscles relax. Had been a while, Bob was assessing me, said,

"You lost some weight there, buddy."

Got that right.

He asked,

"How'd you manage that, I could shed a few pounds . . . what's the secret?"

"Marriage."

He laughed out loud.

I didn't.

Fat people, like people with adopted kids, always tell you up front, get it out in the open and if there's a connection, it escapes me, Bill asked,

"You like Vegas?"

I didn't know, said,

"I don't know."

He enjoyed that, then gave me a rundown on his poker hands. Interesting for all of two minutes, then my eyes began to roam the shelves, seeing brands I'd never heard of . . . what the hell was *ultra dynamite* . . . besides trouble? Then Bill, louder,

"You want a job?"

Took me a moment to register what he was asking, I
echoed,

"A job?"

My amazement blazing through, he began to peel the
label off the long neck, said,

"I have a chain of security agencies with a little private
investigation on the side, all over the country, this climate
of paranoia, business is booming."

I asked the obvious:

"Why me?"

The bartender, unbidden, set up a fresh set of beers, with
bowls of peanuts, chips, even a selection of dips; Bill at-
tacked them with passion, said,

"Couple of reasons; first, because I like you, not that it's
necessary but it helps. Two, you're smart and that definitely is a bonus. Three, you were in the service, know
how to handle yourself, that's a major plus."

I finished my beer, tried not to hear him grind the peanuts and he asked as I smiled,

"What's funny?"

I told the truth.

"A private eye, hadn't figured on that as a career choice."

He selected a chip with great care, had to be the biggest, dipped it in the cream, offered,

"Here, they're good."

I passed, waited, and he added,

"Here's my card, give it some consideration, pay's real fine."

I put it in my wallet, said,

"I don't have a green card."

He wasn't bothered, said,

"Not a problem, am I wrong, you plan on staying State-side?"

"That's the plan."

"So, you're going to need a job, can't see you like . . . what, working a bookstore or some nine-to-five jive."

Tempted to tell him that was exactly what I used to do, I said,

"I've some stuff to get done, then yeah, why not?"

He called to the tender,

"Set us up something special, we're celebrating."

I said,

"I'll stay with beer, that okay?"

He had a bourbon, rocks, asked,

"You want to catch a show, hit the tables, my dime?"

I finished the beer, said

"Love to but there's a couple of calls I should get to."

He had his hand out, said,

"I've to be getting back to Chicago real soon, but here's to a bright future."

I went back to my room, the beer fortifying me, time to call Siobhan, I was up, feeling good, put the call through, waited . . . then heard,

"Yeah?"

A male accent, worse, a Northern Ireland accent.

Stapleton.

Stunned, I tried to regroup, asked,

"The fuck you doing in my house?"

A laugh, then,

"Stevie, we've been worried about you, boy, thought you were never going to call."

I tried for control, the beer not helping at all, asked,

"Where's my girl?"

He made a sound, as if smacking his lips, said,

"Good question . . . she's like, disappeared."

I felt the room spin, tried to focus, shouted,

"If you've hurt her . . ."

"You'd do what, write to me, you need to calm down, big guy, she was here, and let me say . . ."

Pause.

"She's a hell of a fuck, man, she buckled under me like a wild cat, you know that already, of course, I'm getting hard just recalling it."

The wet sound again.

I said,

"She's dead, isn't she?"

He gave a low laugh, then,

"You're a terrible man, always jumping to conclusions, it's that Brit in you, let me ask you something?"

I waited and he went,

"That accent them fuckers have, them Brits, if you gave them a fright really early in the morning, they'd talk normal, do you think?"

Sweat was pouring down my front, I said,

"If you've hurt her . . . "

He gave a sigh, then,

"You're off again, why would we hurt her, she's our leverage . . . for our money."

I couldn't help it, echoed,

"Your money?"

Now he went Barry Fitzgerald mode,

"Sure and whose t'would it be?"

A fun guy.

I said,

"If Siobhan's hurt, you'll never see a bloody cent."

He took a moment, then,

"Am I hearing hostility?"

When I left the black hole, that is, didn't answer, he said,

"The said Siobhan wasn't inclined to chat but eventually, she sang like a blackbird, the money scam, meeting you in Tucson . . . are you still up for that?"

My mind was reeling, I tried,

"And you're planning to tag along?"

He laughed, said,

"Wouldn't miss it for the world, I don't see you returning to us, call it an intuition."

I let my rage flow:

"Bring it on, shithead, I'll be there, waiting for you."

A sigh, as if I disappointed him, then,

"I'm still hearing those negative waves, you need to get a handle on that, boyo."

I crashed the phone down.

Stood, turned on the TV . . . *Friends* . . . I watched without a single reaction. An enclyclopedia salesman was trying to sell a volume to Joey, going,

"How is your general knowledge?"

Seeing Joey's blank face, he tried,

"Where does the Pope live?"

Not missing a beat, Joey replied,

"In the woods."

I switched off, got on the phone, took time, but eventually, got one of Siobhan's friends. Not encouraging, Siobhan hadn't been seen for two weeks, hadn't shown up for work.

After the call, I said aloud,

"She's dead."

But what if she wasn't? She'd no way of contacting me, if she had escaped from them, she'd try to make the Tucson rendezvous. Either way, I'd have to go . . . I wanted to meet Stapelton . . . Jesus, did I ever.

I dialled another number, Siobhan's home. A long shot but if she needed to hide, anything was possible; her father answered, sounded like he always did, gruff, belligerent, drunk. I asked,

"Is Siobhan around?"

"Who?"

"Your daughter, Siobhan, have you seen her?"

A pause and for a brief moment, my spirits lifted . . . maybe . . . then,

"I haven't clapped an eye on her these three years, with a bit of luck, it will be three more."

Closed him down.

The room was oppressive, my mind riddled with poison, I got out of there, walked quickly back to the Sahara, Bob was still at the bar, said,

"Hey, hey, you changed your mind."

I ordered two shots of bourbon, nudged one over to Bob, said,

"I need your help."

He lifted his glass, touched it to mine, said,

"You got it, good buddy."

"info freako"

— VOICE OF THE BEEHIVE

ON WEST GATES PASS ROAD, as Speedway Boulevard winds its way from the city of Tucson, you hit the International Wildlife Museum. Dade was driving, no destination set, speed cranking in his veins, Tammy on the speakers, "Funny Face," he shouted,

"You sing it, babe."

Times like this Tammy was speaking to him, he hit the volume.

No shit, she knew Dade was her man . . . he hit the volume again, the noise near swaying the vehicle, he was driving a pickup . . . Sherry gone to get her hair, as she said,

"Prettied up."

Dade had bought the pickup for eight hundred bucks, from a guy out of El Paso, it was beat up, had serious milage but the sucker moved. All he needed was a hound dog, Hank Williams on the speakers, gun rack, he'd be the complete redneck, the image made him smile, Tammy was onto "I Fall To Pieces."

Dade went,

"Bitching . . . fucking song kills me, darlin'."

He sang along, into it, seeing him and Tammy, heads together, at the microphone, leaning in for each alternate line, high-fiving it to the massive, chanting crowd . . . could hear that crowd, howl,

"Tammy . . Dade . . . Tammy . . . Dade."

He spotted the sign . . . International Wildlife Museum . . . thought why not? . . . jarred to a halt . . . paid seven bucks admission and was seriously pissed, returned to the admission booth, asked,

"The hell kind of scam you running here?"

The woman, bored, focused dull eyes on him, went,

"What?"

"The animals are stuffed, what's that about?"

She gaped at him and he asked,

"Why doesn't it say on the sign . . . 'Dead Animals'? . . . huh, roadkill! I can get in my truck and drive, get all that crap on the side of the goddamn highway?"

She said,

"You want live Mister, you need to get down to the Arizona-Sonora Desert Museum."

She looked at her watch, cautioned,

"Don't go today."

"What, they closed?"

"It's nearly noon, the animals have their siesta."

She refused him a refund and he had a moment, climb in the booth, stuff her, line her up with the other stiffs. Stormed outa there, to see a bum sitting on the kerb, who asked,

"Got any change, buddy?"

Dade kicked him in the side, said,

"Get a fucking job."

Back in the truck, the music died, he seriously lost it, thrashed the panel till his hands hurt, then his cell buzzed, startling him, he got it to his ear, rasped,

"Better be good."

"It's Fer."

Dade hadn't expected him for another week, needed to get Sherry in gear if they were going to take the dude down. Apart from ripping off the guns, the cash, the dope.

Dade just wanted to waste an angel.

Like a country song:

"Wasting the Angel."

He vaguely remembered Sarah McLachlan, she did some tune along those lines, got famous 'cause Clinton gave Monica Lewinsky the album or was it the other way round. His brain was so fried, he couldn't remember, thought

"What . . . the . . . fuck . . . ever."

Bodily fluids had been exchanged, sort of, that's what counted.

Fer grunted,

"You there?"

Dade's head bounced back, he said,

"You betcha."

Mean chuckle from the biker and,

"Y'all been messing with that there mescal?"

Pronounced it mess-cal, a biker's humour, added,

"You all fucked up on that wetback hooch, that it, partner?"

Dade was going to enjoy slamming the Walther in this hog's mouth, said,

"I'm cool, bro, got my shit together, just waiting on da man, waiting on you, *amigo*."

Fer was talking to someone in the background, sounded heated. Dade flashed on the biker chick, the suburban wannabe outlaw, then Fer said,

"We're ready to roll, you got the cash dollars?"

Ready and waiting."

More background debate, then,

"We figure to haul into Tucson tomorrow evening, how's that?"

Dade figured, yeah, get it done, said,

"Cool."

Then Fer said,

"Slight change of venue."

Dade's antennae was up, cautiously he asked,

"Why's that, bro?"

Belly laugh, with,

"Lest you figuring to bushwhack me, try to take me off."

Dade put some hurt in his voice, let a little whine leak over the words, asked,

"You don't trust me?"

The laugh out loud and,

"Man, I don't trust my mom and she's like dead, ten freaking years."

Mom?

They set up the meet at a flophouse off Congress Street. Dade knew of a club nearby, specialised in indie music, suggested that as alternative.

No bite.

Fer wanted the flop joint, and Dade conceded.

When he caught up with Sherry a few hours later, he almost didn't recognise her, her hair was short, coloured brunette, she asked,

"So, you like it?"

He hated it. Before, she'd looked a little like Tammy, now she looked like an accident; he waited a beat too long and she snapped,

"The fuck you know."

He moved to touch her, got his hand slapped away, felt the familiar rage coast, tuned out . . . A moment, refocused, heard,

"Anyway, it's not like it's permanent, just till we get this Irish prick buried."

Dade wondered . . . who?

He asked,

"Who?"

She glared at him, used her down-home voice, the trailer trash out to play:

"Dun tol' you the whole fang, who whacked my ol' man, the prick, he sees me now, he don't know me, he saw a blonde but now . . ."

Back to her own voice:

"I coldcock the sucker."

Dade had forgotten the whole thing, so caught up in partying, it seemed like Sherry had been round forever; he asked,

"What makes you so sure this cat is going to like . . . you know . . . come to town?"

A smile now, a smile of pure maliciousness, her anger

replaced by a lethal certainty, she tapped a smoke, got it in her mouth, lit, exhaled, said,

"He's coming. A young guy who works at the Lazy 8, I slipped him a couple of bucks, keep his eye on the register, new guests, like that."

Dade figured, from that smile, she'd slipped him more than a few bucks, something further as a sweetener and re-alised with horror, as an icicle slid along his spine . . . he was like . . . jealous? The fuck did that happen, and seeing her eyes, knowing she knew. His carefully constructed per-sona, the composite he used to cruise, was flaking away. He needed more dope, felt a pain in his gut, needed vio-lence, managed to ask,

"What makes you so sure he'll show?"

She was stubbing at the cigarette, in the way that women do.

Halfheartedly.

Dab it, maybe twice in the ashtray, short stabbing ges-tures, attention focused elsewhere, leaving the goddamned thing to smoulder, like it no longer had any connection to her. When Dade had done his jolt, the years behind bars, he'd read some psychology book, found it in the yard, first fifty pages shredded, for a spliff or toilet paper more likely, took it back to his cell, began to read it, trying to get a fix on his own self. All sorts of interesting shit, like a man, strikes a match, he strikes in inwards, living recklessly, the flame not a prob-lem. But a chick, always strikes outwards, protective, away.

Dade was fascinated by that detail, somehow realised that in that data was the massive chasm between the sexes. Excited, worked up, he'd shared the info with his cellmate, a supremacist outta the hills of Kentucky. The guy, picking his nose, with intense concentration, said,

"Like, who gives a fuck?"

Chow time, Dade had put powdered glass in the bigot's stew, early in the morning, the cracker on his knees, spitting blood, Dade asking,

"Like, who gives a fuck?"

Sherry said,

"He had CDs delivered yesterday."

Dade was confused, she sighed, explained,

"The Mick, he had stuff posted from New York, so, like, he's arriving . . . soon."

She opened her bag, took out a slip of paper, read,

"The music store, East Village, he likes music, I'll give him some songs, I'll give him some thrills."

Dade blew it off with,

"Don't mean nothing."

Her voice raised, going,

"Over two hundred bucks on CDs? . . . he's coming."

Dade veered another direction, asked,

"You stuck on this guy, that it?"

In a cold exact mimic of Dade's remark, she sneered,

"Don't mean nothing."

He shucked out a cig, got a book of matches, lit up, striking outwards, trying it, didn't work, couldn't do it. She reached over suddenly, fury writ large, snapped it alight, he asked,

"So, what's the deal, why you going to all this trouble, I mean, if the dude don't, like, mean nothin'?"

Got some edge in it, let it sound mean, she got right in

his face, the Juicy Fruit he'd given her, all over his nostrils, her eyes huge, said,

"The fuck walked out on me, upped and left . . . like . . . like I was a one-off!"

Dade went,

"Uh-huh."

She was in front of the mirror, checking her hair, frowning, said,

"Nobody, no two-bit Mick fuck walks on me, not now, not ever."

Dade filed the warning.

"I looked around the bar. There were five men in the bar and no women. I was back in the American streets."

— CHARLES BUKOWSKI, *South of No North*

SLAN GO FOILL.

A common Irish term for "See you later" or . . . "That's it." But there is an undercurrent, depending on the intonation. You hear the old people, at the graveside of a loved one, whisper the words with a sadness beyond articulation. The meaning hangs in the air, dances a little with the sway of the breeze, then is washed away by the rain. A faint echo lingering as the evening falls.

I was standing outside the Bellagio Gallery of Fine Art. The showcase was a collection of old masters: Mantegna, Raphael, Titian, Dürer, Rubens, Rembrandt.

Not what you'd expect in Vegas, right?

Why I loved America, the rules only existed to be reinvented and if dollars could buy a dream, then bring it on. In my head was a DVD I'd watched of Bill Hicks . . . Jesus, his death, what a waste. I'd thought the paintings would part balm my wounded heart. But I'd flitted past them, my awareness of the beauty only intensifying my pain. The very first time, Siobhan, we'd made love, her lying in my arms and she turned her face up to me, asked,

"Will you mind me?"

Siobhan had never, never in her woesome life asked anyone for anything, and careless, without thought, full of afterglow, I said,

"I give you my word."

She'd said,

"I'm going to keep you to that."

What had I been thinking?

Siobhan was dead.

Everything pointed to that conclusion. Still, I'd have to go to Tucson lest she was somehow, against all odds, alive.

So I turned away from art, felt the heat from the desert brush my face, uttered,

"Slan go foill."

An indication of my state of mind, I wanted to be in Brooklyn, to walk Third Avenue, stand on the corner of Fulton and Flatbush, trace the border between downtown and Fort Greene, stroll carefree (as fuckin' if) on Nassau Street to McCarren Park, heading towards the Russian church, open a savings account at The Williamsburg and, in the evening, sit on the bleachers, pop a Bud, watch the neighbourhood kids play stickball.

I missed Brooklyn, how weird is that?

I come from a country steeped in culture and without a backwards glance, I'd have settled in Park Slope.

Or better, head for the Jersey Shore, my Walkman going, Bruce with "American Skin," I'd be wearing a Yankees jacket, baseball cap riding low on my eyes, tan chinos and Docksiders on my feet, sifting the sand with my boat shoes, I'd sing along to the chorus, imagine Patti Scialfa giving me the enigmatic smile.

By fluke, I'd caught a classic episode of *The Sopranos*, when Tony and Christopher set up Adriana to be whacked by Silvio. It was the in-joke that made it so memorable. Silvio is played by Steve Van Zandt, original member of the E Street Band . . . Silvio is late, and Tony hollers,

"Where da fuck you been?"

Christopher, in a tone dripping with venom, says,

"The highway's jammed with broken heroes."

From "Born to Run."

There I'd be, minding my own biz, maybe get lucky, catch a glimpse of Bruce and Patti, out for a saunter with the kids, I'd be cool, go,

"How you doing?"

Not stopping or anything, cool with it, no biggie, try not to hum . . . "Into the Fire."

Come evening, I'd be home, small house with a porch, me mates out there, shooting the shit, maybe catch a rerun of *Monk* on TV Siobhan would shout,

"Dinner in ten . . . you guys okay with burgers?"

She'd have only a hint of the brogue remaining, barely discernible. Me, I'd be deep under the American psyche, below radar, no remnant of the old sod. Just a regular joe, work on my car at the weekend, eat meat loaf on Saturday, shoot pool in the local tavern, hear the local band, a high school kid as babysitter . . . kids? . . . me 'n' Siobhan, always planned on two.

When the boy came of age, I'd bring him out the yard, throw slow ones for him to bat into the net, or shoot a few hoops before supper. In the window, the Stars and Stripes and on the fender of my beat-up Chevy, the logo, "Knicks kick ass."

Let out a long, slow sigh, let the dream dance on the desert air, evaporate over the top of the Sands. Such a weariness enfolded me, soul sickness that choked my breathing. The heat was hitting me hard, and I walked into Circus Circus, thinking of Gretchen Peters's song, "Circus Girl." That didn't help one little bit.

Vegas is the great timeless zone, in the casinos, no clocks, no windows, you stagger out and the sunlight kicks you in the teeth, you wonder, where'd that come from.

Right then, I wanted to suspend time. A waitress, impossibly beautiful, gave me a smile of miraculous perfection, asked,

"What would you like, sir?"

Not her and that was damn straight, said,

"Bottle of Bud, long neck and cold as you got it."

That came and I overtipped her, she gave a gorgeous smile, said,

"You need another, you ask for Cindy."

Don't hold your breath.

I was putting the bills back in my wallet when I saw a tiny pocket I'd never noticed, the secret compartment Tommy had mentioned, I opened it and a scrap of folded paper in there. Unfolded it and it was Tommy's spidery writing, some lines of a poem . . .

Took a long pull at the long neck, it was cold, read,

Legacy
Leave you
The leavings of
An inarticulated thanks
Will to you
The echoes of the lines
As yet . . . un-writ
Term you
The keeper of my conciliatory heart
That heart as mortgage
Hold

My throat felt constricted, my heart like a void, the line about *keeper of my conciliatory heart*. Asked meself, were we reconciled, had we renewed our deep and deepest friendship, did he die knowing I loved him?

One thing was for sure, I hadn't been my brother's keeper.

Later in the day, I realised I'd left the lines with the tip on the counter at the bar.

Seemed fitting, I was unable to hold on to anything.

When I'd asked Bob for help, took me a time to articulate the exact detail, asking is not my gig. Time later, the happy side of bourbon, I said,

"I need a piece."

He laughed, asked,

"You taking down a casino?"

When I didn't respond, he got focused, said,

"You can get anything in Vegas."

And then I smiled, said,

"Prove it."

He stood, a tad unsteady, nodded and was gone.

A full hour till he returned, carrying a McDonald's bag, I asked,

"You got hungry?"

He handed me the bag, said,

"I held the mayo."

Could feel the weight, raised an eyebrow, he said quietly,

"Browning automatic, full clip, ready to roll."

I reached for my wallet, he blew that off, said,

"Just don't tell me about it, okay?"

Seemed fair.

Bruce's song . . . "You're Missing" was reeling in my head, time to head for Tucson, should have been Tombstone but I guess they already had their showdown. I had no plan, only show up, kill Stapleton, keep it simple. 'Course, if he saw me first, I wouldn't need a plan. In my hotel room I packed and wondered how my wife, ex-wife was doing. Jesus, marriages and shootings, this was a low profile? I'd hate to think what would have gone down if I'd been headlining.

Deeply regretted losing Tommy's poems . . . not to mention, Siobhan's life . . . some lines of Tommy's had lodged:

> "Make a go of it
> the roar
> was roared enough
> to be nigh . . . meaningless."

I said aloud,

"Got that bang to rights, buddy."

I zipped the bag, looked round the room, then walked

out quickly. Like the man said, you can buy anything in Vegas, save peace, and perhaps the easiest item was a car. Guys go belly up on the tables, they sell that first. Not much advertising about the men who walk out of the Strip, all that's waiting is the desert.

I bought a Buick, keep the American flag blowing. Dark blue, like my aura, almost new, the salesman said,

"Check under the hood, that engine is primed."

I took his word for it, haggled the price though my heart wasn't in it, got five hundred bucks off the marked one, the salesman grinned:

"You're a player."

Like either of us believed it, I began to drive off the lot, he added,

"You have a full tank of gas, you're good to go."

The American dream, me in my car, top down, Highway 66, times I so wanted to get right under the skin of the very soil and then the Irish in me would whisper,

"The Marlboro man died of cancer."

The radio blasting, country station, Kimmie Rhodes and Willie Nelson with the Waits song "Picture in a Frame."

Beautiful song, darkened my heart that was already in shadow. I'd woken one morning way back, to find Siobhan staring at me, I'd asked,

"You okay?"

Her face a mix of melancholy and longing, she'd nodded, said,

"I love looking at you."

Fuck, how do you respond to that, especially as the feeling is not reciprocated.

Coming out of a deep sleep, I was not at my sharpest,

gave some bland reply, mercifully lost to me, and she asserted,

"I'd stand in the rain to catch a glimpse of you."

Hell.

I'd wanted to go back to sleep, sidestep the whole gig, but no, she continued,

"When I was at school, I was I think . . . eight . . . things were very bad at home, I mean, ferocious and I guess I was suffering from stress."

She laughed.

"Stress! Eight years of age and crushed by worry. In assembly, I wet myself, the headmistress made me stand in front of the school, confess my shame."

Now I was awake, reached for her, but she was somewhere else, not touchable, she continued,

" 'Course, that added to my burden, wet knickers, it became habitual, and I don't need to tell you what the other children were like?"

I tried to hug her but she was rigid, carved in stone, asked,

"The headmistress, you know why she hated me?"

I didn't, couldn't imagine, what would make a grown woman hate a damaged child and Siobhan said,

"Because I was poor."

I definitely had no reply, and she concluded,

"So money, that's the only answer, you want to get seriously even, get seriously rich."

The Count

WHEN I'D ARRIVED back at Siobhan's, she had let out a
tiny scream, seeing blood on my collar, down my left
cheek, and I said quickly,

"It's not mine, it's Tommy's."

She'd gotten a towel, washcloth, cleaned me off, then
poured a large Jameson, said,

"Drink that."

She had to hold the glass to my lips as the aftershock hit.
Tremors lashed my body, I heard small whimpers of anguish and realised they were mine. I told her how it had
gone down. She had her arm round my shoulder, asked,

"Is Stapleton dead?"

I didn't know, said,

"I don't know."

She was all business, asserted we couldn't worry about it
then. For one of the very few times, she made a mistake,

we should have worried and worried a lot. If I'd been less shook, I'd have got in the car, driven back to the spot, gone down the incline, and put at least three bullets in his head.

That evening, she looked at the sacks of cash, asked,

"How much do you think is there?"

I had no idea, said,

"A lot."

We began the count and it took five hours. We began by putting wedges of ten grand in piles and as time went by, got tired, just threw whole batches against the wall. I was drinking beer, a lot of beer, and Siobhan, never a drinker, was putting away vodka like water.

Exhausted, she finally slumped against the wall, her eyes out of focus, said,

"Stephen, there's at least three point five here."

I stared at it, hating it, said,

"More, I'd say."

In noir movies, the couple make love on the mountain of money. We were as close to putting a match to it as it gets. What a fire that would have been.

I said,

"The fucking stuff's bound to be cursed."

"Don't swear, Stephen."

Even then, she was herself. And realising what she said, she began to laugh.

Then she got real serious, said,

"They say if you laugh at the dead, you'll soon join them."

I felt one of those cold shivers walk up my spine, tried to shrug it away, said,

"That's a pishrog, you don't believe in all that old super-stitious crap, come on."

She hand her arms round her shoulders, hugging herself as if she was freezing, said,

"I don't know what I believe, I just don't see me ever spending that money."

I went to her, put my arms round her, tried,

"Sweetheart, you're the one who told me money has no conscience, you're a banker, remember, cash is simply a means of escape."

She bit her lower lip, said,

"I don't think there's any escape from this."

Thinking of the life Siobhan had, I roared,

"You bastards."

I felt now as I felt then, a shuddering rage, a cold fury that those bastards can, with such ease, destroy the life of a child. Alcoholism had blighted mine; Tommy, well, he never had a chance, the euphemism *a broken home* had broken him. His feigned indifference was the sad remnant of a spirit shattered in all the ways that matter.

Was I angry?

You fucking betcha.

As I drove, the radio played Emmylou Harris with her lost song to her lost love, Gram Parsons, "From Boulder to Birmingham." I simmered with ferocity.

The Browning was in the glove compartment, I reached, took it out, understood how guys "go postal," why they climbed a tower and began open season. My skin was burning, my American skin? I squeezed the butt of the gun till my hand ached and the fingers grew numb. A spirit of vengeance was in the atmosphere and I was woven into it.

Hitting top speed, blew along, encapsulated in a case of sheer agitation. Christ, if the highway patrol pulled me over, it wasn't going to look good. As the miles ate away, I intoned the mantra I'd adopted, the promise I'd made to Siobhan, *I'll mind you,* and oh god, I could see, as if she were in front of me, the elfin face she had when I said that, her total delight in the pledge.

I wanted to grab Stapleton, gouge his eyes out, there wasn't torment imaginable that would satisfy me.

The scene of me butting him with the gun and the question . . . why, oh why hadn't I followed through, shouting over the radio,

"In the name of all that's holy, why didn't I kill him?"

Sweat was cascading down my shirt and I eased off the pedal, let the pistol slip to the floor, began to climb back. If I arrived in Tucson like that, he'd eat me alive.

A colder place, I needed to get to that acre in my mind where the flame burned but with cooler heat. I pulled over, counted down from one hundred, got my heartbeat slowed. Took a time, but went from hyperventilation to a zone, if not of peace then less agitation, muttered,

"Okay."

Pete Hamill wrote of Frank Sinatra: "What Sinatra evokes is not strictly urban. It is a very particular American loneliness — that of the self adrift in its pursuit of the destiny of 'me,' and thrown back onto the solitude of it's own restless heart."

I hummed a few bars of "Under My Skin" and was, if not consoled, at least distracted.

"The private terror of the liberal spirit is invariably
suicide, not murder."

—NORMAN MAILER

AFTERWARDS, Dade could never quite fit the sequence of
events in his mind. The quantities of dope and booze in-
gested didn't help. An air of slow motion, of not being part
of it, clung to his assembly of the facts. It had started good.

He and Sherry met with Fer at the dive.

Dade cautioned Sherry,

"Fer has a biker chick with him, you got to watch those
broads, they're sneaky as a rattler, so you get a chance, you
frisk her, make sure she isn't carrying any weapons, we
don't want her producing any surprises when the shit goes
down."

Sherry gave him her most sluttish smile.

"Me, frisking her down, running my hands all over her,
that get you hot?"

He sighed, Sherry was so far out there, he couldn't keep
score, he said nothing.

They were primed for action when they met up with Fer and his woman.

Lots of high fives, tequila and hits of speed. Fer took a real shine to Sherry, she downplaying, goddamn coy, like she was awed by the angel. Kept touching his arm, letting her eyes linger on his crotch and he sucked it up. Fer's old lady was not a happy camper, glared pure poison at Sherry, who smiled sweetly. Dade went to take a piss and Fer followed, unleashing beer torrents. Both sighed contentedly, Fer said,

"Hell of a woman there, partner."

Dade shrugged, said,

"No biggie, just hooked up with the bitch a few days is all."

Fer bought it, asked,

"You guys not an item?"

Dade, zipping up, laughed.

"Nothing to me, bro, piece of trailer trash is all."

When they got back, Sherry had asked Dade to help her select some tunes on the jukebox, Fer said,

"Put some Guns n' Roses on, you hear?"

Sherry said,

"I gave the babe a hug, took her by surprise, hugs are not the gig she's used to, but I got to frisk her good, she's not carrying."

Then Sherry laughed, added.

"She asked me was I was some kind of dyke, me running my hands all over her."

Dade pushed,

"You sure she's clean?'

Sherry smirked, said,

"She hasn't had a bath since Bush took over but no, she's not carrying any weapon, unless you count her foul mouth."

Sherry took a quick look over at the bikers, said,

"Those sure are the ugliest boots I've ever seen on a babe."

And they were, heavy motorcycle jobs, that came to her knees, scuffed and worn.

Many brews later, Fer said, leering at Sherry,

"Let's get down to business."

Dade felt the jolt of adrenaline, time to boogie. They went back to Sherry's villa, Dade and Sherry in the pickup, Fer and his woman behind in a beat-up Dodge. Back there, Fer had Dade help him carry the boxes inside, laid them on the floor, then Fer went out again, returned with a cloth bag, some CDs . . . said,

"Put these on, I like to hear those punks when I'm doing business, and this is my travelling pharmacy."

He spilled the bag out and pills of every colour rained on the floor.

He gestured towards the boxes:

"And there is primo firepower, get your own militia started."

Dade checked the music, the Ramones, put it on, and smiled as he heard the scream, "One, two, three, four," then "Blitzkrieg Bop."

Dade laid out rolls of bills, asked,

"You want to count it?"

Fer gave a full grin, green and gold teeth, a dribble at the corner of his mouth, said,

"Me . . . count it . . . no way, Jose."

And before Dade could respond about trust and shit, Fer pointed at his woman. Said,

"My bitch does that."

He was openly staring at Sherry, stroking his crotch, said,

"Got me an itch here."

Sherry gave a bashful smile, excused herself, said she needed to get something in the bedroom. Fer looked at Dade, who gave him the thumbs-up. Dade, alone with Fer's old lady, asked,

"You like the Ramones?"

They were into "Sheena is a Punk Rocker."

She gave him an icy glare, adjusting those heavy boots she had, as if they were itching her, she said,

"They're dead."

He raised his eyebrows, asked,

"They sound dead to you?"

She was deep into the count . . . still fiddling with the boots and then back to the count muttered,

"Fuck you."

He loved it, asked,

"Get you something?"

Without looking up, she snapped,

"Bourbon, rocks."

There was an almighty roar from the bedroom, the woman, alarmed, looked up, Dade reassured,

"No biggie, she likes her men to howl."

The woman was on her feet, worried as the sound of a body hitting the floor, then the bedroom door opened, Sherry, wearing only panties, covered in blood, staggered out, a knife in her left hand, gasped,

"Gutted, like the pig he was."

Too late, Dade registered the gun in the woman's hand ... had come out of the boots, no wonder she'd been messing with them, having a pistol in there was sure bound to have been a bitch. The gun was in her hands, double grip and squeezing off rounds.

Four shots at Sherry, then turning to him. He dived behind the table, fumbled for his weapon, two rounds slammed into the wall behind him, inches from his face. He'd the Walther up, let off a full clip, the sound deafening him, and heard her fall backwards. Cordite, smoke, and then a stunned silence filled the room. He took a deep breath, stood up, moved to the woman, her head was half gone. Turning towards Sherry, he whispered,

"Tammy, babe, you okay?"

One round in her left eye, he sighed,

"Aw, fuck."

He didn't touch her, went into the bedroom, the angel on the floor, his jeans round his knees, his throat a riot of slashes, Dade moved back to the front room, opened the cloth bag, whistled. A kaleidoscope of dope, he did some crystal, figured he needed something fast, lethal. Waited for the ignition, he was singing quietly,

"Let's get the blanket from the bedroom."

Took him a time to get the bodies into the pickup, then he drove to the desert, buried them deep. Before filling the hole, he'd gotten the photo of Tammy, thrown it in, said,

"Hell of a show, babe."

He drove Fer's Dodge back to the dive, left it there. For the past week, he and Sherry had played music loud and mean to get the neighbours accustomed to raucous behaviour so when the gunplay went down, no cops would be called. Still, he kept a wary eye on the road. Back at the Villa, he opened a bottle of Easy Times, did two rapid shots, then some blow, a little speed and got to work. Cleaned the place from top to bottom, scrubbed the floors, put a fragment of brain in the bin liner, washed the walls, the chemicals in his blood pushing him till his fingers bled. Did another shot of booze, cranked with speed and hopped in the shower, scalded his own self, got a white T . . . with the logo "Twisted City," a fresh-washed pair of Levi's and got the hell out of there. He didn't look back, not a habit he ever acquired. As he drove, he used his bleeding hand to gather the Tammy tapes, threw them out the window, shouted,

"Wreck on the Highway."

A speeding Mack mangled the tapes as it burned towards Phoenix.

The next few days, Dade made plans to offload the spoils. His heart wasn't in it. Without Sherry, he felt at a loss. Sitting in the pickup, running pictures of her in his head when it came to him: *Finish her business for her.*

The Irish guy she'd been expecting, fuck, he'd do it for her. He got in gear, went to the Lazy 8, hung out in the lobby. Two days of this before he choose his mark. One of the bellboys, late twenties, seemed to evade work at every opportunity. His name tag read "Willy." Dade let another day slide by, then when Willy finished work, he followed him. The guy headed straight for the cantina, got a cold one, grabbed a table. Dade got two brews, sauntered over, took a chair, said,

"Howdy, partner."

Willy gave a nod, cautious, Dade stared at him, asked,

"How much you pulling down there, William?"

"What?"

"The Lazy 8, the dead-end gig you got going, with tips, scarce in your case, I'd figure, tops, you're maybe lucky to see two hundred bucks?"

Willy glanced round, see who else was involved, then back to Dade, tried,

"And it's your business, how?"

Put a little muscle in there but it was halfhearted, he'd gotten a look in Dade's eyes, it drained the tone of conviction. Dade laughed, he'd caught the hint of aggression and nothing he loved more, it was low-key mind fucking, kept his act sharp, he said,

"You're the only white guy, what, they weren't hiring at Denny's? All the rest of the help, they're like, wetbacks, can't be easy."

Dade had hit the nerve, Willy's voice rose, "It's only temporary, get me a few bucks stashed, I'm so outta there."

Dade nodded, as if he approved the sentiment, then asserted,

"Like that's ever going to happen."

Willy glared at him, gulped his beer, made to leave, Dade had a hand up, said,

"Whoa, here's a cold one, bring it down a peg, I might be the answer to your dream."

A week later, Dade's cell shrilled and he answered, went,

"Yeah?"

"An Irishman just checked in."

Dade punched the air, asked,

"And?"

"That's it."

"Willy, get up to speed pal, like, room number?"

A pause, Dade could imagine the dollar signs in Willy's eyes, then,

"I don't know, that seems . . ."

"You want the cash or not?"

Got the room number.

Willy's body was found in an alleyway, listed as drug-related homicide, twenty tabs of speed in his jeans.

Dade watched the Irish guy for a few days. Dude had that army stance, and cautious, discreetly clocking everything out. Dade withdrew into the shadows. Come evening, the guy went to a bar, had a couple of shots of Jameson, that shit cost, then walked back to he Lazy 8. Fourth night, Dade was ready. As the guy approached the motel, Dade appeared, staggering, reeling, holding his stomach, the guy let him close, asked,

"You all right?"

Dade sunk the knife in his belly, then with both hands, ripped upwards, bent over the guy, right in his face, the guy's low moan, his hand on Dade's shoulder, lightly, as if he were merely seeking support, then Dade withdrew the blade, pushed it deep into the throat, pulled it lengthways, said,

"It's a country song."

He was about to walk away when he had a thought, bent over the guy, scalped him.

"Life is improvised, it loses its interest when the highest stake in the game of living, life itself, may not be risked."

— SIGMUND FREUD

I ARRIVED in Tucson at midday and was amazed at how flat it seemed, the small buildings like toytown after New York and Vegas. I had to pull over, ask a guy for directions, he warned,

"Lazy 8? You don't wanna go there, buddy."

"Why's that?"

He gave a low whistle, said,

"Bad hood, bad shit happens there, lots of dope."

And moved on. Well, trouble was what I'd come for. Found the place and liked the look if it, a dude ranch. Got my bag, went to reception, the oddest thing happened, my accent arrived.

I was speaking like an American, they confirmed my reservation, handed me the parcel of CDs from the village music store. I asked if Siobhan had shown up, not yet.

Not yet.

I clung to that.

*   *   *

Tucson had been Mexican property until the Gadsden Purchase. I noticed the Mexican influence straight away. I didn't know a whole lot else, save that there was the University of Arizona, the Davis-Monthan Air Force Base, Southern Baptists.

On the drive in I spotted mountain flora nestled right up against cacti. And suburbs, jeez, how many were there and, more importantly, did they ever, like, ever end.

Everybody had transport, from old Caddies to state-of-the art Harleys, to beat-up trucks, yeah, with the rifle on the back window. The pedestrians were but briefly out of their vehicles, and the rest, the rest were Mexican.

All I could think about was,

"How would Siobhan respond to it?"

Followed immediately by,

"Would she be here to do so?"

Made myself focus on the vital issue, find Stapleton.

I'd thought of staying elusive, stalk the neighbourhood, get to Stapleton by stealth. Truth was, I was tired, playing hide and seek wasn't something I could find the energy for. Come evening, I went, had a few drinks, being cautious without being obvious.

The second night, I was coming out of the bar, heard

"Be-jaysus, 'tis himself."

And got a wallop to the side of my head, followed by a kick to the balls, I was down and hurting, bad.

Stapleton.

He hunkered down, grabbed me by my hair, said

"Fooking amateur, I could kill you right now, but thing is, I want me money."

He stood up, in his left hand was a bowie knife, he said,

"On your feet, lad, I need to get you focused, see this knife, I bought it downtown, they have a grand selection in this neck of the woods."

I managed to get up on one knee and get a good look at him, his body was relaxed, the born fighter, the knife loosely held. He'd done this before, a lot, and more, he relished it. The up-close-and-personal gig, that was where he lived. My own time in the British army was going to have to serve me very well now, I tried to get into that zone they had drilled into us but when you've had a kick in the balls, it's a little hard to concentrate, I croaked,

"Where's my girl?"

He mimicked me exactly:

"*My girl*, that's fooking lovely, warms the cockles of me heart."

Then his hand moved and the knife opened a gash on my right cheek, from my eye to my mouth. He said,

"I could have taken your eye, and what would you do, beside piss and moan."

Arizona has lots of dust, gets on your shoes, in your hair, but right now I was glad of it, grabbed a handful and threw it in his eyes, he staggered back and I followed, throwing sucker punches to his kidneys, ribs, and two granite ones to his head. He didn't go down, the bastard was in terrific shape, the slash from the knife to my face kicked in and combined with the agony in my groin, I faltered, lost my advantage, I'm sure if I'd been able to continue my assault,

I'd have killed him there and then with my bare hands.

He used the moment to pull a pistol from his waist, said,

"Whoa, back off, tiger, unless you want the Falls Road special, lose one of your kneecaps."

We were both breathing heavily and he said,

"We got us a Mexican standoff, you think . . . so here's the deal, you bring me the money in twenty-four hours, I'll tell you where to find the girl."

I managed to gasp,

"And what, I'm supposed to trust you?"

He gave a sour laugh, said,

"Like you have a choice."

And he was gone.

I got back to my room, poured whiskey onto the wound and howled, managed to apply a series of Band-Aids to it, took a look at my own self in the mirror. I saw a seriously fucked, desperate face.

Next morning, at breakfast, I'd ordered pancakes, coffee. More caffeine than food. My guts were a knife of tension. A group of Canadians at the next table, I was half listening when I heard,

"Yes, murdered right outside, an Irishman."

I tried not to react, kept still and listened. What I could gather, was, in the early hours of the morning an Irish male had been robbed, knifed to death, he'd been a guest at the motel. I waited but they'd moved on, were planning a trip to Tombstone, see a reenactment of the OK Corral. I went to reception, got directions to the local newspaper office. A girl in her twenties at the desk there, big smile, my accent was holding as she asked,

"You from New York?"

I nodded and she said,

"I want to do a journalism major, I applied to Manhattan, is it like, really exciting?"

I curbed my impatience, said,

"Never sleeps."

She stared into space, imagining the new life, seeing herself in a loft in Chelsea, bagels and lox for breakfast.

Yeah.

Then she focused, asked,

"Sorry, what was that again?"

I repeated my request for the early morning paper. When she got it, I reached for my wallet, she looked behind her, said,

"No charge."

I put the stuff under my arm, said,

"See you on Coney Island."

I read the paper with a sense of shock, relief, agitation, and disappointment. The accounts reported how an Irishman, identified from his wallet as a John A. Stapleton, had been robbed and murdered. Police had been unable to find relatives or family of the deceased. A spokesman for the Tucson cops said they were treating it as mugging gone wrong. Finally, they were pursuing a definite line of inquiry.

Bollocks.

They had nothing.

The next few days I spent in a state of disbelief, couldn't accept he was dead. Was life so random that he'd run into a mugger and was taken by surprise. 'Course, he would have been less alert than usual, after our encounter. Didn't think I'd ever have the answer. Frustrated, I rang Mike, who owned the music store I'd worked in. He was amazed to hear me and sounded . . . cautious? Went,

"Steve, good lord . . . where are you?"

By rote, I said,

"London."

Silence and I had to prompt,

"Mike, you still there?"

"Yes, I'm . . . I don't know what to say."

I tried,

"It's okay, I'm fine."

"She was a lovely girl, I'm so sorry."

Oh god, sweet Jesus, I asked,

"What did you say?"

He took a deep breath,

"When she, sorry, Siobhan, when her body washed up on the beach, we were stunned."

I put the phone against my forehead, needing a moment, cold sweat was popping out in streams, heard Mike go.

"Steve?"

I struggled to keep my voice in check, asked,

"Was there an inquest, did it say it was drowning?"

He sounded gutted, went,

"The coroner called it 'death by misadventure.' "

What a fucking term, when they don't know if it's foul play or suicide, they apply that meaningless description. Like, what? Siobhan's great adventure went astray? I said,

"Thanks, Mike, sorry to put you through this."

Concern in his tone, he asked,

"You going to be okay?"

"Yeah, sure."

He hesitated, then risked,

"It's just, you have an American accent."

I could have laughed, finally got under the skin, said,

"Talk to you soon."

Hung up.

They buried Stapleton in the local cemetery, nobody had come forth to claim him. I went to visit, stood over the freshly turned clay, spat on it, said,

"You cheated me."

I'd wanted the showdown, an old style settling of a blood feud. I'd sworn that the next meeting with him, I'd be ready and one of us was going to die.

I wondered who prayed for Siobhan, it was far too late for my pleas.

Rang Bob, told him my business in Arizona was done, he asked,

"Did you use, the item from Vegas?"

"No, never came to that."

"Good, you still want to work for me?"

"Sure."

I heard him rustle some papers, then,

"We have a client in New York, he thinks someone is going to kill him"

"Is he right?"

"Well, why you don't fly up there, ensure it doesn't happen."

"Now?"

"Unless you have a reason to stay where you are?"

I thought about it, said,

"No, I've no reason to stay."

I made a call to Mike at the music shop, asked him a

large favour, said I'd send the necessary money to cover the request, he said it wouldn't be easy, they didn't allow burials outside the city limits, I sealed the discussion by upping the amount.

I had a terrible phone call to make, would have put it off if I could have thought of any way out, but it had to be done.

To ring Kaitlin.

I sat on my bed in the motel, arranging the script and it wouldn't write. My hands were covered in sweat. I'd a fifth of bourbon on the table, poured a double, knocked it back. Didn't ease the dread. Dialled the number and she answered almost immediately, I said,

"Kaitlin, it's Steve."

And oh god, she sounded full of life. Energy and warmth pouring from the phone, saying where the hell were we and why hadn't Siobhan called her, I stopped her, said,

"I've some bad news."

"Bad, how bad, are you all right?"

Fuck.

I said,

"It's Siobhan."

And could hear the instant concern in her tone, she near roared,

"Is she sick, I'll come, you tell her I'll —"

"She's dead, Kaitlin."

A pause, the longest I've ever endured, and then the disbelief . . .

"Dead, how can she be dead, not Siobhan, Sweet Jesus, tell me it's not true."

I could hear the sobbing, the rising hysteria in her, said,

"I wish it weren't true, Kaitlin, I'm so sorry."

Could hear the repeated flick of a lighter and she wailed,

"Why can't I light this bloody cigarette?"

I suggested she get a drink, and on the spur she asked,

"You having one?"

Like we were in a bar, buying rounds, like it was normal, caught unawares, I said,

"I've a large bourbon in my hand."

She screamed,

"A drink, like that's going to help, tell me what happened!"

I tried to choose my words, said,

"They said that —"

And she roared,

"They . . . who the fuck is *they*, isn't she with you . . . God almighty, wasn't, wasn't she with you?"

"No, it happened in Ireland."

Her breathing sounded raw, ragged, and she said,

"Just tell me."

"They . . . I mean . . . am . . . she drowned, an accident, I'm sure."

Enraged her, she went,

"You're not even sure of what happened, what's wrong with you?"

Good question. I said,

"I'm sure she's dead."

"You promised to mind her, you promised me, you gave me your fucking word, didn't you, didn't you promise?"

Her weeping was horrendous, I said,

"Yes, I promised, I'm so sorry."

She let loose a torrent of abuse, recrimination, interspersed with sighs of such pain that I felt as if she were physically assaulting me, that would have been preferable to what I was hearing. I was holding the phone so tightly that it cut into my palm. In my torment I said,

"If there's anything I can do?"

Christ, talk about the wrong selection of words . . .

Ice in her tone now, she mimicked,

"Do? Maybe you could give me your word, but there is one thing you can do."

I grasped at it like a slim prayer, said,

"Anything."

"You can roast in hell."

Banged the phone down.

My whole body was shaking and I thought,

"Oh yes, that I can do, I'm already most of the way there."

An odd encounter after I checked out of the Lazy 8. I was waiting for a cab to take me to the airport. A pickup stopped, the engine still running, a guy hopped out, swinging the door carelessly, if I hadn't stepped back, it would have hit me. I said,

"Jaysus, take it easy, you nearly whacked me."

He stared at me, a curious expression flitted over his face, he scratched a scar shaped like a sheet of lightning on his cheek.

He stared at the Band-Aids clustered on my cheek, then he shook his head, said,

"My mistake, partner."

He walked towards the rear of the motel, his boots clacking against the concrete, the heels in need of repair.

He reminded me of someone, I was in the cab when I got it, Christopher Walken . . . then I forgot about him.

Dade was on his second beer when he realised what was niggling at him. The dude, outside the Lazy 8, his accent, was there a trace of Irish in it? He shrugged it off, thinking,

"Two Irishmen at the Lazy 8, naw, couldn't be."

But it wouldn't go away, so he stalked the motel again, got himself another bellboy, laid out the bucks and discovered yes, the second guy had an Irish passport though he spoke like a New Yorker. Got the dude's name, Stephen Blake, mail to be forwarded to the Milford Plaza, New York. And yes, he had had a package of CDs sent from New York. An old song by Tammy, "Please Come to Boston," began to unreel in his head.

He changed Boston to New York, began to hum that.

My second day back in New York, darkness had such a hold on me, I thought I'd never see the light again. I'd made contact with the businessman who felt his life was in danger, was due to meet him later in the day. Agitated, broken, I was walking, found myself on the bridge over the Hudson, the thought of suicide was strong, join Siobhan. Almost automatically, I reached to my neck, unclasped the chain and fingered the gold Miraculous Medal, as if somehow it would connect me to the spirit of Siobhan.

Then I raised it in my fist, hurled it high, it glittered for one brief, fiery moment, then dropped into the water.

It was such a tiny thing, I didn't really expect it to make a splash, but I waited, then turned and began to stride away, the sound of my new Arizona boots cracking on the asphalt . . . the whisper on the Manhattan wind . . . *dead man walking.*

On a small hillside, a half hour's drive from Galway City, overlooking the bay, there is a granite headstone, it overlooks the spot where Tommy's body stands sentinel against the cold Atlantic. Takes a lot of juice to have a burial there, for juice, translate as money, lot of it.

The headstone is new and catches the light as the sun dips from the west. Lights up the few lines inscribed there:

"Mind her well."

If you were of a dark frame of mind, you'd almost think it's irony.

It's certainly a knife in the heart.